秘书系列

高职高专工作过程导向新理念规划教材

涉外秘书英语

韩乃臣　主　编

付梦蕤　郝　帅　翁亚玲　倪洪源　副主编

清华大学出版社

北　京

内 容 简 介

本书以高等职业教育应用英语专业涉外文秘方向的学生就业为导向,在行业专家的指导下,贯彻以"学生"为中心,以"实践"为核心,以"项目"为载体,以"企业"参与为平台的原则,致力于打造高标准的职业方向课程教材。本教材以一个虚拟的项目贯穿于整个课程。贯穿项目由课程模块体现,每个模块下设子项目,由这些子项目来构成整个贯穿项目。全书共分 18 个单元,各单元内容既自成一体,又互相联系。每个单元包括 Warming-Up, Introduction to the Topic, Situational Dialogue, Practice, Course Project 五个环节。

本书适合高职高专文秘专业学生作为职业英语课程的教材使用,也适合社会企业文秘人员、行政管理人员自学。

图书在版编目(CIP)数据

涉外秘书英语/韩乃臣主编 . —北京:清华大学出版社,2011.3
(高职高专工作过程导向新理念规划教材. 秘书系列)
ISBN 978-7-302-24640-4

Ⅰ.①涉… Ⅱ.①韩… Ⅲ.①秘书－英语－高等学校:技术学校－教材 Ⅳ.①H31

中国版本图书馆 CIP 数据核字(2011)第 013751 号

责任编辑:刘士平
责任校对:袁 芳
责任印制:孟凡玉

出版发行:清华大学出版社   地   址:北京清华大学学研大厦 A 座
         http://www.tup.com.cn   邮   编:100084
         社 总 机:010-62770175   邮   购:010-62786544
         投稿与读者服务:010-62776969,c-service@tup.tsinghua.edu.cn
         质 量 反 馈:010-62772015,zhiliang@tup.tsinghua.edu.cn

印 装 者:北京市清华园胶印厂

经   销:全国新华书店

开   本:185×260   印 张:10   字 数:226 千字

版   次:2011 年 3 月第 1 版   印   次:2011 年 3 月第 1 次印刷

印   数:1~3000

定   价:24.00 元

产品编号:037521-01

前 言

　　随着我国国际化进程的日益加快，尤其是加入 WTO 之后，商务工作人员，特别是涉外企事业单位工作人员对英语语言知识的需求更加迫切。作为高层管理人员的助手，涉外企事业单位的秘书及行政助理人员对英语能力的要求越来越高，要求他们必须具备用行业英语顺利地进行口头和笔头的对外交流和内部沟通的能力。

　　《涉外秘书英语》是以高职应用英语专业涉外文秘方向的学生就业为导向，在行业专家的指导下，通过对行业及企业的调研和与学院专业教学指导委员会研讨，编者确定了涉外秘书英语教材编写的总体原则：以"学生"为中心，以"实践"为核心，以"项目"为载体，以"企业"参与为平台，致力于打造高标准的职业方向课程教材。

　　本教材以一个虚拟的项目贯穿于整个课程，全书共分为 18 个单元，各单元内容既自成一体，又互相联系。每个单元包括 Warming-Up，Introduction to the Topic，Situational Dialogue，Practice，Course Project 五个环节。贯穿全书的整体项目是：Rachel 经过面试被格瑞特文具有限公司（Great Stationery Co.，Ltd.）聘为总裁张先生的秘书，经过培训后正式开始了其秘书工作。在此期间，公司的供应商布瑞杰文具公司（Bridge Stationery Co.，Ltd.）和公司的英国客户 Officemate Trading Co.，Ltd. 先后来访，而格瑞特公司总裁张先生要去参加广交会。本教材以 Rachel 在格瑞特公司的秘书工作过程作为贯穿全教材的项目，全方位、全过程模拟秘书的全部工作过程。

　　全书内容具体包括：

　　(1) Rachel 参加格瑞特公司的工作面试。

　　(2) 格瑞特公司对其进行岗位培训（包括秘书职责、礼仪、公司历史、公司结构、办公设备使用方法等）。

　　(3) 正式上岗后的日常内部、外部口头交流，如与同事、上级、供应商和英国客户的电话交流、指示与请求、商务会议等。

　　(4) 日常公司内部、外部书面交流，与同事、上级、供应商和英国客户的函电、会议记录、备忘录、商务报告等。

　　(5) 来访接待。Rachel 需要全程负责接待先后来访的布瑞杰文具公司销售代表陈小姐和 Officemate 的首席执行官 Paul King 先生，包括接机、订酒店、参观公司、介绍公司及其产品、商务宴请等。

　　(6) 安排商务旅行。Rachel 需要为其总裁张先生参加广交会做好安排，如预订酒店房间、预订机票、行程安排等。

本书具有以下特色：

第一，注重培养学生的综合实践能力。语言材料真实，训练项目以真实工作岗位需求来设计，充分体现了高职教育"实用为主、够用为度"的原则。

第二，贯穿项目由多个子项目组成，子项目中又有"任务型"角色扮演来体现，从而完全改变了以知识为主线的传统编写体系。真正实现了对学生职业能力的培养，充分体现了高职高专英语教学改革的方向。

建议在使用本教材的过程中，专业教师和企业人员共同完成授课任务。这样学生不仅可以从教师那里学到专业知识，还可以从企业人员那里学到真实的技能操作，了解工作流程。这种教学模式体现了校企合作的原则，有利于学生了解企业情况，为就业打下良好的基础。

由于编者水平有限，编写内容难免有不妥之处，恳请专家、同行和读者批评指正。

编　者

2011 年 1 月

Contents
目　录

Project 1

Job Interview

Task 1   Picture recognition.

How time flies! You (Rachel and Robert) will be graduating this June. You will be facing the problems of looking for a job. However, there are thousands of kinds of jobs available in the world. Do you know all of them? Now have a try! Please identify what jobs they are in the picture below.

A. (   )

B. (   )

C. (   )

D. (   )

E. (   )

F. (   )

Task 2   Matching.

Are you really preparing for job hunting? What kind of preparation should you do before you start your job interview? Listed below are some things you need to get ready or familiar before your job interview. Try to match the Chinese phrases in the right column with their English version in the left column.

1. certificate
2. job vacancy
3. prospective employer
4. job duties
5. requirements for applicants
6. major competitor
7. major market
8. want ad
9. diploma
10. cover letter
11. application form
12. reasons for hiring
13. corporate culture
14. curriculum vitae
15. telephone screening
16. shortlist

a. 求职简历
b. 求职信
c. 毕业文凭
d. 证书
e. 职位空缺
f. 招聘广告
g. 潜在招聘方
h. 应聘条件
i. 应聘表
j. 工作职责
k. 主要市场
l. 主要竞争公司
m. 招聘原因
n. 企业文化
o. 电话筛选
p. 最后候选人名单

II. Introduction to the Topic

Five Steps to Get a Job[①]

Step 1—Career Planning and Management

Before you embark on your job hunt, you need to be clear about what you want for your career. Planning does not mean going on the job hunt yet. It simply means that you start the planning, and you should, before you are ready to look for a job. When you are actually ready to look for a job, you may not have the time or the resources to plan for your career then.

You need to approach your career planning holistically, because there are many factors that affect your career decisions. Some key factors are your skills, interests, wants, values and constraints. By having a composite approach to your career planning, you mitigate the possibility of making a biased decision, thereby having to change your mind too often.

The key to your career planning is to know what you like, rather than what you are good at. Many questions such an approach, thinking that career management is an airy-fairy

---

① Source: http://www.docstoc.com/docs/13651674/The-Job-Hunting-Process, 2010-12-30

subject. Truth is you do need to balance your interest with the need of the real world. It is not a unilateral decision only. You must balance what you like with what the world needs. How much to compromise will depend on your needs at the moment. An example of such an approach is that when you are young, you will probably be more willing to give up more of your personal time for a more lucrative job. But as you get older and start a family, you may want a more balanced lifestyle, thereby reducing your willingness to compromise on your personal time for work.

For many, they make the mistake of just knowing what the world wants, without knowing their own likes. The world may have a need. But if you do not see yourself in that area of work, will you be willing to compromise your likes to accept a career in that area? Start with your likes, and see how much you may have to compromise, to reach the "ideal" career for yourself.

Step 2—Job Hunting

Looking for a job in today's market is different from what it used to be. When there were more jobs than people available, minimal effort in a job hunt may still result in a successful job placement. Gone are the days when you will need to fight off offers from executive search even while you are gamely employed.

Today, writing to many hiring managers may not result in any reply. The whole job hunting process is taking much longer and becoming more demanding and tedious.

To be successful in a job hunt today, you need to employ all the sources in finding a job. Newspapers continue to be a good source of indicating hiring patterns, and the skills that employers want. Job agencies and executive searches may be hard pressed for entry level or low end jobs, unless part-time, temporary or hourly-waged. Job fairs outside of schools are also more for low-end jobs. The best method in job hunting today is via networking.

Job Hunting Process

1. Career Planning & Management → 2. Job Hunting → 3. Strategising → 4. Resume & Cover Letter Writing → 5. Interviewing

Networking takes time and effort. Networking is not about connecting with your contacts on whether they have any job available for you. Networking is NOT a short term effort to land a job, but an on-going process to know more about the jobs, companies and industries you wish to apply for. The value of the networking is in gaining information for competitive advantage to get to the job of your desire.

Step 3—Strategising

Upon finding the job that you want, it is almost time to get the job application going. But before the job application, you will need to do some strategising.

The purpose of the strategising is to give your job hunt a focus. In today's tight employment market, the key is to be focused. Not focused on what you want to show the hiring managers, but what the hiring managers want to hear from you.

Instead of focusing on what are your strengths, and all your achievements, the focus is on how your strengths and achievements can be repeated to benefit the job you are applying for.

Develop a list of about six to eight requirements that you think are essential to the job you are applying for. The accuracy of this list will be based on your ability to network. If you have networked well, you will have little difficulty coming up with an accurate list.

Your job hunt, from resume and cover letter to the interview, will depend on this competency list.

Step 4—Resume and Cover Letter Writing

Upon getting a focus on your job hunt, you are now ready to write your resume and cover letter. Similar to the Strategising Step, the focus is on what the hiring manger wants, rather than what you wish to show the hiring manager.

What you have achieved to be recorded into your resume cannot be changed. What are your previous experiences? What school did you attend and what degree did you attain? What did you do in school, awards attained, co-curriculum activities, or projects completed? These things would not change. What have been done have already been done. How you describe these achievements according to what the hiring manager would like to see must be customised for each job, company and industry. So, the resume and cover letter are not about your features, as many have the misconception, but how your features can benefit the job, company and industry. As such, understanding the job, company and industry is essential, which goes back to your competency list (Step 3—Strategising) and your networking (Step 2—Job Hunting).

Step 5—Interviewing

Interviewing is about communication, the ability to connect with the interviewer(s). Paying attention to every aspect of communication would be a good idea. Many are not aware of their non-verbal and voice-control communications.

Other than noting the communication, preparing for the interview is similarly overlooked. Knowing more about the job, company and industry before you go for the interview will give you added advantage. Furthermore, working on the answers that you would give during an interview would be useful.

It is difficult to think and speak at the Peter time. Rehearsing your answers thoroughly so that you can communicate with your interviewer(s) during the interview rather than only answering the questions will certainly be a useful aspect of the interview.

Throughout the interview, it is important to remind the interview(s) why you are suitable for the job, company and industry, rather than just answering his/her questions.

Exercise: True or False

1. _____ You are not ready for a job hunt if you have not thought about your career planning.

2. _____ If you only think about your interests, you will not make a good career planning.

3. _____ As soon as one has found an appropriate job, he or she should go applying for it immediately.

4. _____ Your work experience in your resume should be the same for all targeted job.

5. _____ If you know more about the prospective employer, you have better chances to get the job.

Ⅲ. Situational Dialogue

Ms. Snow, the personnel manager with an advertising agency, is interviewing Peter Li, a job applicant. The whole job interview is divided into 4 parts below.

Dialogue 1　Greeting and personal information

Peter: Excuse me, may I see Ms. Snow, the personnel manager?

Snow: It's me. What can I do for you?

Peter: I have come at your invitation for an interview. Nice to meet you, Ms. Snow.

Snow: Nice to meet you, too. Please sit down.

Peter: Thank you.

Snow: May I have your name?

Peter: My name is Peter Li.

Snow: OK, Mr. Li, we have received your letter in answer to our advertisement. I would like to talk with you regarding your qualifications for this position.

Peter: I am very happy that I am qualified for interview.

Snow: Where do you live now?

Peter: I live at 78 Zhongshan Road, Ningbo.

Snow: Are you a permanent resident of Ningbo?

Peter: No, I am only a temporary resident. I am originally from Hunan, but I have lived in Ningbo for 6 years.

Snow: What is your greatest strength?

Peter: I think I am very good at planning. I manage my time perfectly so that I can always get things done on time.

Snow: What are your weak points?

Peter: When I think something is right, I will stick to that. Sometimes it sounds a little stubborn but I am now trying to find a balance between insistence and compromise.

Snow: What are your greatest accomplishments?

Peter: Although I feel my greatest accomplishments are still ahead of me, I am proud of my involvement with the International Business Conference'93 project. I made my contribution as part of that team and learned a lot in the process.

Snow: Can you work under pressure?

Peter: Yes, I find it stimulating. However, I believe in planning and proper management of my time reduce panic deadlines.

Dialogue 2   Talking about educational background

Snow: Would you tell me what educational background you have?

Peter: Yes, I graduated from middle school in 2002, and then I entered Ningbo Polytechnic. I graduated in 2006 with a B. S. degree.

Snow: What department did you study in?

Peter: I was in the Department of Physics.

Snow: How were your scores at college?

Peter: They were all excellent.

Snow: What course did you like best?

Peter: I was very interested in Business Management. And I think it's very useful for my present work.

Snow: How are you getting on with your studies?

Peter: I'm doing well at school.

Snow: Which subject are you least interested in?

Peter: I think it was Chinese History. Not because the subject was boring, but the large amount of material that have to be memorized. It left no room to appreciate the wisdom of great people in the past.

Snow: When and where did you receive your MBA degree?

Peter: I received my MBA degree from Peking University in 2008.

Snow: Were you in a leading position when you were a college student?

Peter: Yes, I was president of Student Union of our university, and I joined the Communist Party of China in my junior year.

Snow: Did you get any honors or awards at your university?

Peter: Yes, I got the university scholarship in academic year 2004 - 2005, received the second-class award in the Olympic Mathematics Competition of our province in 2000.

Snow: Great. Were you involved in any club activities at your university?

Peter: Yes, I was at the college basketball team.

Snow: What extracurricular activities did you usually take part in at your college?

Peter: I persisted in jogging every morning. I sometimes played table tennis and sometimes played basketball.

Dialogue 3　Talking about work experience

Snow： Have you got any experience in advertising?

Peter： Yes, I have been working in the Public Relation Section of a company in the past two years. I plan the advertising campaign and cooperate the work of artists and typographer. Sometimes I have to do the work of a specialist when there's something urgent.

Snow： Have you had any experience with computers?

Peter： Yes, I studied in a computer training program, and can process data through the computer.

Snow： That's fine. What about operating the fax and duplicator?

Peter： I can handle them without any trouble.

Snow： How often do you work overtime?

Peter： I worked overtime several times a month.

Ⅳ. Practice

Practice 1　Who are qualified?

You just found on a website a job ad, which is shown below, looking for an HR Officer/Assistant. Some of your friends are interested in this position, but you have got different educational background and work experience. Read the job ad carefully, especially its requirements part, and find out who among the following people are qualified candidates. Tick the qualified candidates.

Human Resources Officer/Assistant(大连市)

Main Responsibilities

1. Be responsible for the administration of social benefits and commercial insurances
2. Proceed the employment and termination for local and expatriate staff
3. Perform full scope of recruitment function including experienced hiring and campus recruitment
4. Prepare management reports

Requirements

1. Degree holder in Human Resources Management or related from university
2. 1 – 2 years practical HR experience preferably gained in a multinational company
3. Well versed with the labor laws and the employment related laws
4. Strong inter-personal and communication skill with high proficiency in English (both written and spoken)

(　　) **Tom**，a high school dropout，with 5 years experience in a private company.

(　　) **Bill**，a college graduate majoring HR Management，having worked as an assistant to HR Manager for 3 years.

(　　) **Buddy**，a Harvard Law School graduate with some internship with world-known law offices. Very familiar with labor laws.

(　　) **Christina**，a veteran sales with several Fortune 500 companies. Especially good at communicating with customers both in written and spoken ways.

(　　) **Michael**，a green hand with an MA degree，majoring in labor laws.

Practice 2　Group discussion

Whether a job interview is successful or not depends on many things. Of course, interviewees' C. V. , cover letter, their educational background, and work experience count the most, but there are some other minor factors that can also make a difference between a success and a failure. Talk to your partner and decide which ones of the following factors are important in a job interview and explain why. You can supplement some other aspects you think are important.

(1) outward appearance (dress or face-painting)

(2) speak with smile

(3) body language

(4) come on time

(5) others：

_____

_____

_____

Practice 3　Tough questions and smart answers

During a job interview, interviewers often ask interviewees some tough questions or some sensitive questions about your shortcomings. It is very important for you to handle embarrassing situation and turn it to your advantage in the end. The following lists of questions are some tough questions we may encounter during the interview. With your partner together try to answer them reasonably and wisely. Then try to think of other tough questions and ask your partner to answer them.

● Why have you changed your job so often?

_____

● Why did you quit?

_____

● How long have you been out of work?

_____

- What have you been doing during this period?

  _____

- What do you think about your former boss?

  _____

- What are your salary expectations?

  _____

- How long are you expecting to work with our company?

  _____

- What is the biggest mistake you have made during your previous work?

  _____

- What should the company do to you if you make the same mistake or similar mistakes
  again?

  _____

Other Questions

_____

_____

_____

V. Course Project

You are Rachel and Robert, two English majors from Ningbo Polytechnic. You will be
graduating this June. You are interested in working as a secretary in a foreign company.
Now, start your job hunting.

Task 1

Rachel and Robert just found two job ads, one from PricewaterhouseCoopers, another
from Great Stationary Co., Ltd. Discuss together and decide which one is suitable for
them, and explain your reasons.

Job ad 1

Job Description & Responsibilities
- Provide secretarial support to HR Staff Services Centre(SSC)leader and managers
- Organize/make conference meeting arragements
- Take meeting minutes
- Prepare and organize meeting materials(e. g. Agenda, PowerPoint presentation, Excel spreadsheet...)
- Provide communication coordination & handle client phone query
- Make calendar arrangements
- Make travel arrangements(travel itineraries and hotel reservation)

- Prepare expense reimbursements
- Make co-ordination of SSC internal communication & staff activity(e. g. birthday celebration, team gathering events); and
- Take up other ad-hoc assignments

Requirements

- University degree
- At least three years' experience on secretarial or administrative role in multinational companies; overseas study or work experience a plus
- Good English language skills (speaking, listening, writing, and reading)
- Aptitude in standard computer software, including Word, Excel and PowerPoint
- Multi-tasking and hard working with a high level of commitment
- Good inter-personal and communication skills
- Friendly attitude-cheerful and diligent
- Self-motivater, well-organized, and good problem solving skills
- The ability and willingness to build positive working relationship with team members.

Job ad 2

Great Stationary Co., Ltd.

Report Line: Great China CEO

Responsibility

- Liaise, assort with Internal & external information
- English translation(Oral and Written)
- Organize and scheme company meeting seminar exhibition
- Note important meeting & draw out document draft
- Travel arrangements
- Travel & entertainment report preparation
- Arrangements for visitors
- General filing

Personal Qualities

- Enthusiastic, positive attitude
- Good interpersonal skills
- Good potentialities and plasticities
- Sense of urgency and priority

Skills

- Proficient computer skill with common MS software, Strong at PPT and Excel is a must
- Good Command of written and cralenglish
- Good time management

After your ad reading and discussion, your decision is: _____

And your reasons for your decision are:

_____

_____

Task 2

Suppose you have decided to apply for the second job, the one with Great Stationary Co. , Ltd. Now you need to get your C. V. and cover letter ready. Follow the advice in Part Ⅲ. Write your own C. V. and cover letter based on your own information. You can make up some information if necessary, e. g. work experience.

Task 3

Now you have received an invitation by Great Stationary to its job interview. Work in pairs to role-play the whole job interview process. The following aspects are required to be involved in your dialogue:

(a) personal information
(b) job objective
(c) qualification
(d) educational background
(e) work experience
(f) skills & hobbies

Project 2
Job Duties

Task 1   Discuss the following pictures concerning job duties as a secretary.

A. (   )   B. (   )   C. (   )

D. (   )   E. (   )   F. (   )

Task 2   Translate the following expressions into Chinese.

1. clerical   _____
2. routine   _____
3. reservation   _____

4. newsletter _____

5. administrative _____

6. transfer call _____

7. take dictation _____

8. arrange meeting _____

9. draft correspondence _____

10. schedule appointment _____

11. take shorthand _____

12. confidential files _____

13. management functions _____

14. coordinate work _____

15. tidy up documents _____

Ⅱ. Introduction to the Topic

Job Duties of Company Secretaries

Company secretaries are responsible for ensuring that their company complies with standard financial and legal practice and maintains standards of corporate governance. Although they are not strictly required to provide legal advice, company secretaries must have a thorough understanding of the laws that affect their areas of work. They act as a point of communication between the board of directors and company shareholders, reporting in a timely and accurate manner on company procedures and developments.

Public limited companies are legally required to employ a company secretary and most private companies also appoint into the role. Positions can be found across all sectors and in the public sector this role often has the title "chartered secretary".

Typical work activities

A company secretary's role covers a wide variety of functions and these depend, in part, on the company for which they work. Typical work activities, however, include:

● organizing, preparing agenda for, and taking minutes of board meetings and annual general meetings (AGMs);

● maintaining statutory books, including registers of members, directors and secretaries;

● dealing with correspondence, collating information and writing reports, ensuring decisions made are communicated to the relevant company stakeholders;

● contributing to meeting discussions as and when required, and advising members of the legal, governance, accounting and tax implications of proposed policies;

● monitoring changes in relevant legislation and the regulatory environment, and taking appropriate action;

- liaising with external regulators and advisers, such as lawyers and auditors;
- taking responsibility for the health and safety of employees and managing matters related to insurance and property;
- developing and overseeing the systems that ensure the company complies with all applicable codes, as well as its legal and statutory requirements.

The work of a company secretary in a registered company may be more specialized than in a smaller private company. For example, the liaison role with shareholders and compliance responsibilities may make up a major part of the work and may include:

- maintaining the register of shareholders and monitoring changes in share ownership of the company;
- paying dividends and managing share option schemes;
- taking a role in share issues, mergers and takeovers.

In small businesses, other duties commonly undertaken by company secretaries include:

- monitoring the administration of the company's pension scheme;
- overseeing and renewing insurance cover for employees, equipment and premises;
- entering into contractual agreements with suppliers and customers;
- managing office space and property and dealing with personnel administration;
- overseeing public relations and aspects of financial management.

Exercise: True or False

1. _____ Company secretaries are strictly required to provide legal advice.
2. _____ Companies are legally required to employ a company secretary.
3. _____ A company secretary in a registered company may be more specialized than in a smaller private company.
4. _____ A secretary plays an important function as the liaison role with shareholders.
5. _____ The company for which the secretary work decides secretary's variety of functions.

Ⅲ. Situational Dialogue

Sara is the secretary of Mr. Zhang, the sales manager in ABC company.

Dialogue 1

Sara: Excuse me, are you Mr. Dong Hua?

Dong: Yes, I am.

Sara: How do you do, Mr. Dong? I'm Sara Li, Mr. Zhang's secretary. I'm here to meet you on behalf of our manager.

Dong: How do you do, Miss Li. That's very kind of you. Thank you for meeting me at the airport.

Sara： It's my pleasure. Did you have a pleasant trip, Mr. Dong?

Dong： Not really, I'm afraid. I was a little dizzy on the plane.

Sara： I'm sorry to hear that. Are you feeling better now, Mr. Dong?

Dong： Yes, I'm much better now.

Sara： Do you have a hotel accommodation, Mr. Dong?

Dong： Yes, I have reserved a single room at the Great Wall Hotel.

Sara： Good. Shall we head to the hotel now, our driver is waiting outside.

Dong： Great! Let's go.

Dialogue 2

Sara： Excuse me, are you Miss Liu from the People's Insurance Company of China?

Liu： Yes, I am. You must be Sara Li, from ABC Company, am I right?

Sara： Yes. Welcome to Chongqing, Miss Liu. I'm here to meet you on behalf of our manager, Mr. Zhang.

Liu： That's very kind of you. Thank you very much.

Sara： How was your trip, Miss Liu?

Liu： Wonderful! I haven't traveled by train for a long time. I found it quite interesting.

Sara： Great! By the way, do you have a hotel accommodation, Miss Liu?

Liu： Yes. I have reserved a single room in the Friendship Hotel. How shall we go to the hotel?

Sara： By taxi. May I help you with your luggage?

Liu： Yes, thank you. You are so kind, Miss Liu.

Dialogue 3

Sara： Good morning, Sir. Can I help you?

Tao： I'd like to see Mr. Zhang. I have something important to tell him.

Sara： I'm sorry, Sir. Mr. Zhang is not in right now.

Tao： When will he come back?

Sara： He won't be back until 2 o'clock in the afternoon. Would you mind waiting?

Tao： I'm afraid I can't. Can you give me the number of his mobile phone? It's very urgent.

Sara： I'm very sorry, sir. I don't know his number.

Tao： What a pity! Can I leave a message?

Sara： Yes, of course.

Tao： Please tell him to call me back as soon as possible. My name is Tao Jianguo. My number is 139xxxx5231.

Sara： No problem, Sir. I'll make sure he gets the message.

Tao： Thank you, Miss. Good-bye.

Sara：Good-bye.

Ⅳ. Practice

Practice 1   Arranging a meeting

Student A：You are the secretary of Mr. White (your boss), who wants to have a meeting with the buyer from ABC company. You are asked to arrange the meeting. Except Saturday and Sunday when your boss is in Hongkong for a meeting, you are supposed to arrange the meeting this week or next week if the buyer is not free this week.

Student B：You are the buyer of ABC company and you are free only on Sunday this week. You suggest having the meeting at Hongxing Hotel next Monday afternoon.

Practice 2   Meeting customer at airport

Student A：You (Mr. Richard) are the customer from CCA Company in America. You come to China to visit Mr. White and you just arrived at the airport.

Student B：You are the secretary of Mr. White and you are asked to meet Mr. Richard at the airport and drive him to the hotel.

Practice 3   In the sample room

Student A：You (Mr. Richard) are the customer from CCA Company in America. You come to Mr. White's company and visit the sample room for your purchase.

Student B：You are the secretary of Mr. White and you show Mr. Richard around the sample room.

Ⅴ. Course Project

Task 1

One customer comes to the office to visit your boss, Mr. Zhang without any appointment. Since Mr. Zhang is out, you receive the guest in the reception room and arrange the appointment.

Task 2

The customer, Mr. Johnson from Canada is flying to China to visit your company and you

are the secretary on behalf of your boss to meet Mr. Johnson at the airport. You are supposed to make a poster with the customer's name and his company name (ABC Company,
Canada) on it.

Task 3

Your boss is going to Hongkong for a 3-day trip. The first two days are for business meeting and the last day for recreation. He wants to visit the most popular tourist attraction
nearby. Now you are supposed to arrange the timetable for him, especially the lastday recreation activities.

Project 3
Company History and Corporate Culture

Ⅰ. Warming-Up

Task 1   Picture recognition.

Look at the following slogans and answer the questions below.
- Whose slogans are they?
- What products or services are they associated with?
- Are they well-known in your country?
- Which logos are the most famous in your country?
- Why are slogans important?
- What do these slogans imply?
- Which companies' corporate culture do you know?

WE DO CHICKEN RIGHT

Live For **Dream**
贏　得　夢　想

THE POWER OF IDEAS

Everything starts with an idea. Lenovo PCs help bring them to life.

Task 2　Discuss the desired company culture.

Different companies in different industries will have different cultures. Here are tips for describing the characteristics of company culture. Discuss in your opinion what kind of a culture will work best.

- Customer-focused
- Employee commitment
- High integrity workplace
- Strong trust relationships
- Highly effective leadership
- High degree of adaptability
- Fully empowered employees
- High accountability standards
- Effective systems and processes
- Effective 360-degree communications
- Demonstrated support for innovation
- Commitment to learning and skill development
- Performance-based compensation and reward programs
- Emphasis on recruiting and retaining outstanding employees
- …

Ⅱ. Introduction to the Topic

Company Culture[①]

A culture is the values and practices shared by the members of the group. Company

---

① Source：http：//management. about. com/cs/generalmanagement/a/companyculture. htm，2010-12-30

culture, therefore, is the shared values and practices of the company's employees.

Company culture is important because it can make or break your company. Companies with an adaptive culture that is aligned to their business goals routinely outperform their competitors. Some studies report the difference at 200% or more. To achieve results like this for your organization, you have to figure out what your culture is, decide what it should be, and move everyone toward the desired culture.

Company cultures evolve and they change over time. As employee leave the company and replacements are hired the company culture will change. If it is a strong culture, it may not change much. However, since each new employee brings their own values and practices to the group the culture will change, at least a little. As the company matures from a startup to a more established company, the company culture will change. As the environment in which the company operates (the laws, regulations, business climate, etc.) changes, the company culture will also change.

These changes may be positive, or they may not. The changes in company culture may be intended, but often they are unintended. They may be major changes or minor ones. The company culture will change and it is important to be aware of the changes.

There are many ways to assess your company culture. There are consultants who will do it for you, for a fee. The easiest way to assess your company's culture is to look around. How do the employees act; what do they do? Look for common behaviors and visible symbols.

Listen. Listen to your employees, your suppliers, and your customers. Pay attention to what is written about your company, in print and online. These will also give you clues as to what your company's culture really is.

Exercise: True or False

1. _____Company culture is the value held by its founder, or its boss.
2. _____ Company culture is important because a bad culture can never lead the company anywhere.
3. _____ Company culture is fixed as soon as it was founded.
4. _____ You have to find out your company culture by yourself.
5. _____ The easiest way to assess your company's culture is to ask your management.

III. Situational Dialogue

Dialogue 1　Getting familiar with your office

Ada Brown is a new sales representative with CDE company. On her first day in that company, Jessica Simpson is showing her around their office building.

Ada: Hi, my name is Ada.

Jessica: Ada Brown, the new sales representative? Nice to meet you! I'm Jessica Simpson.

Ada: Nice to meet you, Jessica, but...

Jessica: No buts about it. Now, let me show you around. This is our reception area, and our conference room is right over there.

Ada: This is a nice office.

Jessica: We don't really like it—but don't tell the management. Now, over here is the sales department.

Ada: Really? It's quite small.

Jessica: Yeah, I guess we haven't made enough money to get a bigger space. You can make copies and send faxes over here.

Ada: It sounds like you guys work hard.

Jessica: Not really. We just mess things up so that it looks like we work hard. Now, your cubicle is there, but first, the most important room...

Ada: What's that?

Jessica: Why, the break room, of course.

Ada: Hmm, this isn't a bad way to learn about the company.

Dialogue 2　Nokia Corporation's history

A just got a job in the world famous company—Nokia Corporation as a secretary. On his first day there, B, his department manager, is introducing the company's history to him.

A: As far as I know, Nokia Corporation has a very long history. Then when exactly was it founded?

B: What is known today as Nokia was established in 1865 as a wood-pulp mill by Knut Fredrik Idestam on the banks of the Tammerkoski rapids in the town of Tampere, in south-western Finland. The company was later relocated to the town of Nokia by the Nokianvirta river, which had better resources for hydropower production. That is where the company got the name that it still uses today. The name Nokia originated from the river which flowed through the town. The river itself, Nokianvirta, was named after the old Finnish word originally meaning a dark, furry animal that was locally known as the Nokia.

A: I see. So the company has a 145-year-long history.

B: That's right.

A: But as you just mentioned, the company started as a wood-pulp mill. It had nothing to do with mobile phones. Then when did it start its mobile phone business?

B: That is a long story too during which some round of merge and acquisition (M&A) happened. First, shortly after World War I, a rubber manufacturer called Finnish

Rubber Works, which was established in the beginning of 20th century nearby and began using Nokia as its brand, acquired Nokia Wood Mills as well as Finnish Cable Works, a producer of telephone and telegraph cables. These three companies were merged to form Nokia Corporation in 1967.

A: Did Nokia Corporation start to produce its mobile phones then?

B: Not yet. The new company was involved in many sectors, producing at one time or another paper products, bicycle and car tires, footwear (including Wellington boots), personal computers, communications cables, televisions, electricity generation machinery, capacitors, aluminium, etc. Nokia had been producing commercial and military mobile radio communications technology since the 1960s. Since 1964 Nokia had developed VHF-radio simultaneously with Solora Oy, which later in 1971 also developed the ARP-phone. In 1979 the merger of these two companies resulted in the establishment of Mobira Oy. Mobira began developing mobile phones for the Nordic Mobile Telephony (NMT) network standard that went online in the 1980s and in 1982 it introduced its first car phone, the Mobira Senator for NMT 450 networks. Nokia bought Solora Oy in 1984 and now owning 100% of the company, changed the company's telecommunication branch name to Nokia-Mobira Oy. Then, in 1989, Nokia Mobira Oy became Nokia Mobile Phones and in 1991 the first GSM phone was launched.

A: Woow, it is complicated!

B: I know. This is just the beginning part of its history. Now, Nokia Corporation is a Finnish multinational communications corporation, headquartered in Keilaniemi, Espoo, a city neighboring Finland's capital Helsinki. Nokia is focused on wireless and wired telecommunications, with 112,262 employees in 120 countries, sales in more than 150 countries and global annual revenue of 51.1 billion euros and operating profit of 8.0 billion as of 2007. It is the world's largest manufacturer of mobile telephones: its global device market share was about 39% in Q1 of 2008.

A: Gee! I am very proud of being a part of it.

Dialogue 3 Corporate culture

B, a job hunter, is consulting A about how to fit into a company's corporate culture.

A: Hi, how can I help you?

B: Could you tell me why corporate culture is important for a job applicant when choosing a job and could you give me some advices about how to fit into a company's corporate culture?

A: I'd like to give you an example. Jack Sullivan couldn't have been happier after landing his dream job. The position, salary and perks were exactly what he was looking for. But after the initial happiness wore off, he discovered that going to work was becoming the same daily routine all over again. Although he couldn't put his finger on exactly what was wrong, he knew one thing for sure: he was not comfortable in his new job.

B: What went wrong?

A: Jack did not fit in with the company's corporate culture, which is no surprise, given that company's culture—the beliefs, attitudes and behaviors that commonly unite its employees—is often unstated and unwritten.

B: Does the company have a stated set of cultural values?

A: Progressive companies are aware of corporate culture's influence and have thought about the values they want to promote in their organizations. If the company has no written cultural values, ask to see the mission statement, which should also provide some insights into this area.

B: What does it take for someone to be successful here?

A: First of all, he should know what kind of personal characteristics the company is looking for? Risk-taking? Entrepreneurial spirit? A team player? Then take note of personality traits that are encouraged and rewarded and think about company culture. Asking this question early in the job interview also allows you to incorporate these sought-after characteristics into you answer.

B: What kind of employee achievements are recognized by the company?

A: Again the answer to this question will reflect the company's values and rewards systems.

B: How do you understand the environment?

A: Well, listen to the adjectives the interviewer uses. What aspects of working there does he or she choose to talk about—the camaraderie among employees, the career development opportunities or the free breakfast bar?

B: How often are company meetings held?

A: This is a good question. Are meetings held weekly? Monthly? Yearly? Who attend? What does this say about the priority management gives to keeping its employees informed? This is what matters to the culture of the company.

B: How about the physical layout?

A: Are special rooms delineated as "team" rooms for collaborative work or brainstorming? Does the layout promote or discourage interaction between departments? Different style of the office will create different cultures.

B: How about the overall impression of the place?

A: From the dress code to the door code, can you picture yourself working there? What does your gut say about becoming part of this company? Although you can survive a bad fit in a company's culture, why endure a mismatch when you could be thriving elsewhere? For many people, work is more than a paycheck; it is where they meet their friends or spouse, spend most of their waking hours and define their personal identity. So make sure it's not just a company where you can work, but a company that works for you.

IV. Practice

Practice 1   Cloze

There are 15 blanks in the following passage. For each blank there are 3 choices marked A, B, and C on the right side of the paper. You should choose the ONE that best fits into the passage.

Nike History [①]

The Shoe Game's favorite company would have to be Nike. Nike was __1__ in 1962, by Bill Bowerman and Phil Knight __2__ started as Blue Ribbon Sports. It wasn't until 1972, when they __3__ to call their upcoming company "Nike", which was __4__ after the winged Greek goddess of victory. After reading that you would think Nike's logo would be a wing, but __5__ Nike went with the "Swoosh". The "Swoosh" is well known all around the globe, and it was __6__ in 1971, by Carolyn Davidson for ONLY $35.00. Not only can Nike be spotted by the "Swoosh" logo, it's well known "Just Do It" __7__ makes Nike stand out like no other company.

It took a while for Nike to establish the great name they have today, and in the early 80's many people complained about how Nikes were not made in the United States (US). People were mad at the fact Nike shoes were made in Vietnam, China, and Indonesia where the people are __8__ in low wages and treated __9__. This led to a major __10__ with Nike products, leading to boycotts. Although, this was a major issue to some people it didn't stop Nike from handling business.

The major turning __11__ for Nike was when the world's greatest basketball player came to the company in 1985. Michael Jordan changed the game and it took Nike to another __12__ with the popular "Air Jordan" shoe along with the apparel. Nike may never admit to this, but Mike is greatly responsible for their __13__ today. Without Mike, Nike probably would __14__ be trying to get to the top, but "Thank God" for Michael Jordan.

Later on down the line Nike teamed up with more famous __15__ like Bo Jackson, Andre Agassi, Charles Barkley, Deion Sanders, Ken Griffey, Scottie Pippen, Penny Hardaway, Jason Kidd, Barry Sanders, and many more.

1. A. found   B. founded   C. built
2. A. originally   B. previously   C. preciously
3. A. changed   B. decided   C. determined
4. A. called   B. given   C. named

---

① Source: http://theshoegame.com/Nike-History.html, 2010-12-30

5. A. instead   B. still   C. even
6. A. established   B. invented   C. designed
7. A. sign   B. logo   C. slogan
8. A. given   B. paid   C. compensated
9. A. poorly   B. well   C. greatly
10. A. fight   B. conflict   C. clash
11. A. feature   B. incident   C. point
12. A. level   B. layer   C. grade
13. A. failure   B. accomplishment   C. success
14. A. still   B. even   C. merely
15. A. players   B. stars   C. athletes

Practice 2   Role-Play

Work in pairs. Each one surf on the internet and find out some information about a world-famous company's history and corporate culture, and ask each other questions about the company to fill in the grids below. Then try to guess the name of your partner's company.

Information	Company A	Company B
Founded		
Founder		
Location		
Activity		
Famous products		
Major markets		
Market share		
Major competitors		
Headquarters		
No. of employees		
Key date		
Annual revenue		
Global presence		
Your guess(company name)		

Practice 3   Presentation

Each student choose a world-famous company, and then go to its website and get some information about its corporate culture, its vision, its value, its responsibilities, etc. Then make a presentation to the class, introducing the company's corporate culture, and explaining how the company has developed its corporate culture. For example, what does Nokia's "Connecting People" mean? Why did Nokia choose this phrase as its corporate culture?

Ⅴ. Course Project

In the previous projects, Rachel and Robert have started their new employee training, and have understood their job duties and etiquette as secretaries. In this project, they will be familiarized by their manager, Mr. Zhang concerning the history and corporate culture of Great Stationary Co., Ltd.

Task 1

Student A: You are the manager of Great Stationary Co., Ltd., Mr. Zhang. You get on the company's website and get some information about the company's history, and then introduce its history to the new secretaries, Rachel and Robert. You might need to answer their questions about the company's history.

Student B: You are the new secretaries, Rachel and Robert. Your manager, Mr. Zhang, is introducing the company's history to you. You are expected to find out the key dates, founder, location, activity, major products, major markets, market share, major competitors, headquarters, number of employees, etc. Then you are expected to retell the company's history to other classmates.

Task 2

You are expected to come up with a logo for Great Stationary. Go talk with your manager, Mr. Zhang about your ideas and tell him why you chose your logo.

Task 3

Miss Chen, the sales representative of your supplier, Bridge Stationery Co., Ltd. is visiting your company. As requested by your manager, Mr. Zhang, you are showing Miss Chen around your company while introducing your company's history, logo, and corporate culture to her.

Project 4
Company Organizational Structure

Ⅰ. Warming-Up

Task 1   Chart recognition.

Look at the organization chart below, and then try describing the company structure.

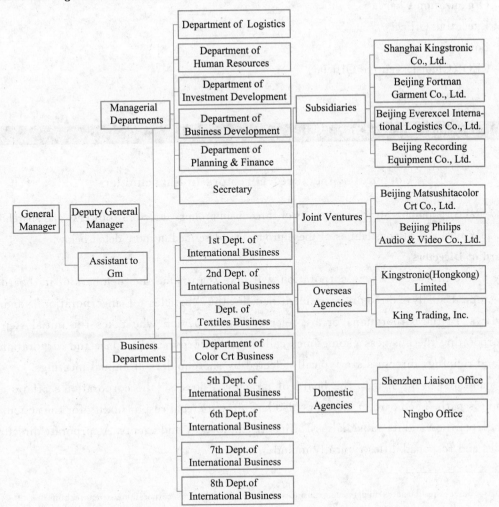

Task 2 Translation.

Translate the following expressions into Chinese.

1. chairman $\underline{\hspace{5cm}}$
2. headquarter $\underline{\hspace{5cm}}$
3. shareholder $\underline{\hspace{5cm}}$
4. reception $\underline{\hspace{5cm}}$
5. manager $\underline{\hspace{5cm}}$
6. Personnel Dept $\underline{\hspace{5cm}}$
7. Marketing Dept $\underline{\hspace{5cm}}$
8. Production Dept $\underline{\hspace{5cm}}$
9. Purchasing Dept $\underline{\hspace{5cm}}$
10. Sales Department $\underline{\hspace{5cm}}$
11. R & D Department $\underline{\hspace{5cm}}$
12. Organization Chart $\underline{\hspace{5cm}}$
13. Executive Officer $\underline{\hspace{5cm}}$
14. Board of Directors $\underline{\hspace{5cm}}$
15. CEO (Chief Executive Official) $\underline{\hspace{5cm}}$

II. Introduction to the Topic.

Corporate Structure: Directors to Shareholders[①]

A typical corporation's structure consists of three main groups: directors, officers, and shareholders. The roles and responsibilities of these groups are described in more detail below.

Board of Directors

One of the first steps a new corporation will take is to name the members of its board of directors. Usually, directors are identified in the "articles of incorporation" and/or "bylaws" of the corporation, or are selected by the person who takes the initial step of incorporating the business (sometimes called the "incorporator"). Once the corporation is up and running, directors are typically elected by shareholders at annual meetings.

As suggested by its name, the board of directors "directs" the corporation's affairs and business path. The board of directors also has ultimate legal responsibility for the actions of the corporation and its subsidiaries, officers, employees, and agents. A corporate director's duties and responsibilities typically include:

---

① Source: smallbusiness. findlaw. com/business-structures/corporations/corporations-structure. html

- acting on behalf of the corporation and its best interests with an appropriate "duty of care" at all times;
- acting with loyalty to the corporation and its shareholders;
- participating in regular meetings of the board of directors;
- approving certain corporate activities and transactions—including contracts and agreements; election of new corporate officers; asset purchases and sales, approval of new corporate policies; and more;
- amending the corporation's bylaws or articles of incorporation.

The number of directors serving on a corporation's board usually depends in part on the size of the business and its holdings, but this number is typically stated in the corporation's articles of incorporation and/or bylaws. A small corporation might have one director (who may also serve as the sole officer and shareholder), while a large corporation may have 10 or more people serving on its board of directors. For voting purposes, a corporation with more than one director should keep an odd number (3, 5, 7, etc.) of directors on its board.

Corporate Officers

The corporation's officers oversee the business' daily operations, and in their different roles they are given legal authority to act on the corporation's behalf in almost all lawful business-related activities. Officers are usually appointed by the corporation's board of directors, and while specific positions may vary from one corporation to another.

Keep in mind that in smaller corporations, one person may serve as the business' sole director, officer, and shareholder.

Shareholders

A corporation's shareholders have an ownership interest in the company, by having money invested in the corporation. A "share" is an apportioned ownership interest in the corporation, and the value of a single share can range from less than a 1% interest in the corporation, to 100%.

When a corporation is first formed, its original owners are usually its first shareholders, and in smaller corporations these initial investors may remain the sole shareholders throughout the corporation's existence. A smaller corporation's few shareholders may consist of those involved in day-to-day business operations (as owners, managers or employees). Remember that in smaller corporations, one person may also serve as the business's sole director, officer, and shareholder. Where larger corporations are concerned, private investors (or members of the general public if the corporation "goes public") may decide to invest money in the corporation at any time, and will become shareholders. Whatever the number of shareholders in a corporation, each shareholder usually receives a stock certificate from the corporation, identifying the number of shares held by the investor.

Corporations are usually required by law to hold annual shareholder meetings, at which the shareholders will elect the corporation's directors. Special shareholder meetings may also be held in rare situations, when significant corporate actions require shareholder approval—including major transactions and changes in the corporation's stock plans. A corporation's articles of incorporation (combined with state law requirements) usually set forth shareholder voting rights and procedures.

Provisions for executive, managerial, and administrative matters are also normally accounted for in a corporate structure, so that everyone in the organization knows where a given issue should be addressed.

Along with providing reference points for the handling of various functions, a corporate structure also helps to establish a line of communication for employees to utilize. This makes it possible for comments, questions, and ideas to flow easily from anywhere in the organization to someone with authority to act on the information effectively. By establishing this line of communication, the corporate structure helps to ensure effective interaction and also minimize time wasted by information moving through the company in a disorganized manner.

Lastly, the corporate structure helps to establish a working chain or line of authority. Corporations often require responsible persons placed at various points in the structure to ensure tasks are handled properly and in accordance with company bylaws. By granting specific levels of authority to persons all along the corporate structure, including making persons accountable to other persons for their competency in exercising authority, it provides a check and balance system to keep the company on an even keel. Employees who are disgruntled with immediate supervisors have someone who can hear their grievances, while overseers may step in and conduct the tasks assigned to an employee when needed.

Exercise: True or False

1. _____ Directors of board are completely elected by shareholders.
2. _____ Board of directors has to take full legal responsibility for the corporation's actions.
3. _____ The size of the business partly decides the number of directors of a corporation's board.
4. _____ The corporation's officers are given legal authority to act in all lawful business-related activities on behalf of the corporation.
5. _____ The initial investors are usually its first shareholders of the corporation, and in smaller corporations when a corporation is first formed.

Ⅲ. Situational Dialogue

Dialogue 1 Organization chart

Rachel is new department manager with ABC company, and her colleague, Mr. Zhang, is

showing her around the company and introducing the company's organization chart to her.

Rachel: Mr. Zhang, what's that?

Zhang: Well, that is the chart showing our company's organizational structure.

Rachel: Could you tell me something about it?

Zhang: OK. On the top, Mr. Thomas, the Managing Director, is responsible for running the company.

Rachel: How many departments do we have?

Zhang: We recently divided the company into three major divisions: Operations, Marketing and Sales, and Finance and Administration.

Rachel: Customer Service is a part of Marketing and Sales?

Zhang: Yes. The Marketing and Sales division has a number of departments: Customer Service, Advertising, Communications, and, of course, Sales and Marketing.

Rachel: And Operations?

Zhang: Operations division is made up of Manufacturing, Materials, Shipping and Distribution, MIS, R&D and I am the Department Manager of distribution, so I directly report to Mr. White, the Director of Operations Division. He is on a business trip and is supposed to be back this morning. Probably you will be meeting him at lunch.

Rachel: OK! Whom should I report to?

Zhang: Mr. White too, because your department—R&D also comes under Operations!

Rachel: And the department managers report to the directors, who report to the CEO?

Zhang: Right. Now, keep in mind that the directors often compete with each other to be in good standing with the CEO.

Rachel: I guess it would be helpful to make your division look as good as possible in the eyes of the CEO.

Zhang: Hmm—now you're getting it. Oh, here comes the CEO.

Dialogue 2

Mr. Zhang is still showing Rachel around the company.

Zhang: Finance and Administration includes various departments such as Accounting, Tax, Payroll, Investor Relations, Human Resources.

Rachel: Where are most of our products manufactured?

Zhang: We have facilities in the USA, Mexico, and Malaysia. Check our company's intranet. You'll find information all about our company's operations, among other things.

Rachel: As a Customer Service Manager, I'd like to think we sell qualified products.

Zhang: Ever since we worked with the MIS department to develop an online quality control program, we've seen defect rated plummet and reliability rates soar.

Zhang： Need to fill you in on what role you will play as the Customer Service Manager.

Rachel： I'm all ears.

Zhang： Customer Services is responsible for professionally handing off customer requests. To do that you'll need to learn how to use our internal system, all of which are on our network.

Rachel： I'm a quick learner. Will I receive any training?

Zhang： MIS worked with Finance and Human Resources to put every procedure, from customer orders to payroll on our website. We have training classes every Tuesday afternoon.

Rachel： Everything's online, hum? MIS must be an important department.

Zhang： Yes, MIS is increasing the productivity of our company with the use of the latest ERP systems.

Rachel： Interesting. I never thought about it that way.

Dialogue 3　The structures of American companies

Lili is a Chinese student in a business school, and she is talking to her American friend, Tom, on Skype, about the structures of American companies.

Lili： Tom, do you know anything about the structures of American companies?

Tom： I know some. What do you want to know?

Lili： Who is higher, the President or the Chairman?

Tom： The Chairman. He calls for the Board Meeting, which makes all the important decisions for the company.

Lili： Does the Board decide who is the President?

Tom： Yes.

Lili： What does the President do?

Tom： He runs the company. He would pick the Vice Presidents.

Lili： How many Vice Presidents does a company have?

Tom： That depends on the size of the company. Big companies like Ford may have hundreds of Vice Presidents.

Lili： Wow. That's a lot. What do they do?

Tom： Who knows? A joke said that you might need a Vice President for parking.

Lili： Ha-ha. It's funny. The directors are under the Vice President?

Tom： Yes, unless he is in the Board of Directors.

Lili： Directors have managers reporting to them?

Tom： Right. You already know a lot.

Lili： Just a little.

IV. Practice

Practice 1

In business world, there are some abbreviations for some titles, some of which are listed below. What do these abbreviations stand for, and what are the job duties of each job title?

1. CEO   2. CFO   3. VP   4. GM
5. COO   6. CTO   7. PR   8. HR

Practice 2   Filling in the blanks

Most large companies have different departments. Fill in the blanks in the following sentences by deciding where these people usually work.

1. Accounts work in the _____ department.
2. Scientists often work for _____ department.
3. Salesperson works in _____ department.
4. Lawyers work in _____ department.
5. PR people is under _____ department.
6. Training Managers are in charge of _____ department.'

Practice 3   Presentation

Work in groups. Each one choose a local company, draw up its organization chart and show the chart to the group, and describe the company's organization structure to the group while other members ask some questions about the company's organization structure, for example,

- the board of directors and the staff
- the department structure of the company
- the job duties of all departments
- the cooperation among different departments
- the future development and plans
- …

V. Course Project

In this project, Rachel and Robert will continue their training. Today, their manager, Mr. Zhang will introduce the organization structure of Great Stationary Co., Ltd.

Task 1

Work in pairs to role-play the situation. One is the manager, Mr. Zhang, who should get on the company's website and get some information about the company's organization structure and then introduce it to his/her partner. The other is the new secretary, Rachel or Robert, who is expected to try to understand the company's organization structure, and ask some questions when necessary then draw an organization chart like the one in Part I for the company.

Task 2

Miss Chen, the sales representative of your supplier, Bridge Stationery Co., Ltd. is visiting your company. As requested by your manager, Mr. Zhang, you are showing Miss Chen around your company while introducing your company's organization structure to her.

Task 3

You are still introducing your company structure to visiting Miss Chen. Now Miss Chen is interested in what each department in your company is responsible for. Explain the job responsibilities of each department to her.

Project 5
Office Equipment

Task 1　Picture recognition.

Shown below are some office equipment that are commonly used in modern offices. Please consult your dictionary to find out their English names.

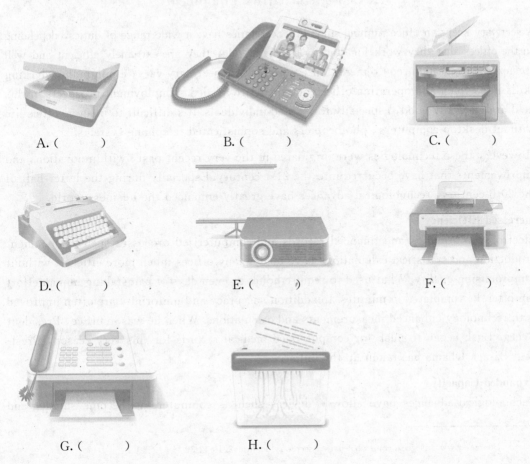

A. (　　　)　　　　B. (　　　)　　　　C. (　　　)

D. (　　　)　　　　E. (　　　)　　　　F. (　　　)

G. (　　　)　　　　H. (　　　)

Task 2 Matching.

Match the English words and phrases with their Chinese counterparts.

1. Interphones   a. 投影幕
2. Office Paper   b. 视听系统
3. Storage Cabinets   c. 门禁设备
4. Security Safes   d. 对讲机
5. Projector Screens   e. 保险箱
6. Visual & Audio System   f. 电子白板
7. Time Card Machines   g. 办公用纸
8. Electronic Whiteboards   h. 储物柜
9. All-in-One Printing Machines   i. 印刷一体机
10. Attendance & Access System   j. 考勤机

Ⅱ. Introduction to the Topic

Advantages of Office Equipment[①]

A secretary keeps an office running smoothly. Secretaries have a wide range of duties, depending on the offices that they work for, but as a general rule, they are extremely efficient and well organized. Qualification requirements for a position as a secretary vary; a minimum, clerking skills like typing and operating office equipment are needed. Employment prospects in this field are generally good, especially for skilled individuals. It's difficult to imagine office life without desktop computers, photocopiers and sophisticated telephone systems.

However, these technologies were originated in the very recent past, with innovations and improvements that have occurred into the 21st century. Especially during the latter half of the 20th century, technological advances have greatly enhanced the business world.

Increased Efficiency
Electronic information and financial records and computerized processes such as document production and statistical calculations have made many offices much more efficient without compromising quality. What used to require hours or even days of painstaking human effort can often be completed in minutes. In addition, accuracy and uniformity are often improved with technology-enhanced measurements and calculations. When he was in office, President George Bush began to push for computerized medical records for this very reason, President Barack Obama has taken up the initiative.

Expanded Capacity
Technological advances have allowed devices such as computers to become smaller and

---

① Source: www. wisegeek. com/what-does-a-secretary-do. htm, 2010-12-30

more effective, and eventually to become a necessity to nearly every business. Instant messaging, the Internet, internal telephone systems and Intranets (internal networks) and especially E-mail are integral to the workings of office life, yet each only came into common use during the latter part of the 20th century. These technological advances have made it possible to transmit enormous data more quickly to lots of people than workers during the early 20th century eventhough possible.

Enhanced Flexibility and Capability

In 2007, 12 million employees worked more than 8 hours per week via telecommuting, according to Gartner Dataquest and reported on MSNBC. Virtual assistants and telecommuters can be located across town or across the world, thanks to the wonders of modern telephone systems and electronic communications. Web conferencing and virtual-world webinars make it possible for colleagues within a company or from different companies to interact with one another in real time. On a more individual level, electronic document production and calculations make it possible to implement small or even major changes, as well as make corrections quickly and seamlessly.

Exercise: True or False

1. _____ Typing is the minimum requirement for a secretary.
2. _____ Modern office equipment has increased office efficiency at the expense of quality.
3. _____ E-mails didn't come into common use until the latter part of the 20th century.
4. _____ Electronic communications has made working at home possible.
5. _____ If a secretary cannot use internet, her employment prospects in this field are generally terrible.

Ⅲ. Situational Dialogue

Dialogue 1　Do you want a computer at work

Mike is doing market research by asking some office clerk whether they want a computer at work.

Mike: Anne, as a secretary, what do you think about the introduction of computers into office life?

Anne: I don't know. I think you are being pushed into a different world—a keyboard world. It takes away the role of secretary. Towards the end of the day you may feel that you have unplugged yourself.

Mike: And you, Sven, as an office administrator, what do you think?

Sven: I'm not very sure. All our bosses have them on their desks but they don't use them. Senior management tend to think that if they install a computer system in their offices and give their staff a couple of days' training, amazing new levels of efficiency will be attained. But that's not true. At first things may get even worse.

Mike：What about you, Mark? You are a bank clerk.

Mark：I think it's very economical. Computers are good time-saving devices. But I'm convinced that we are far from having exhausted the possibilities computers offer to us. We're probably using only one third of their capacity.

Sven：I don't agree with you. Computers have made my life more difficult. It seems that without organizing office work differently, introducing computers doesn't help much.

Mary：I would want one. As a typist, a computer can help me a lot. I can use the keyboard to type in information. The monitor shows what you type so you can correct mistakes very easily. Then the printer quickly produces what you need. They are excellent for storing information on a disk.

Dialogue 2 How to operate the shredder?

A：Can you show me how to operate the shredder?

B：Certainly. It's easy. First, press the green button on the right side of the machine to switch it on. You have to wait for half a minute before you can put waste paper into it, because it takes the shredder a while to warm up and then get ready.

A：OK, I can wait. Then what should I do?

B：Then, just put the paper you would like to shred into the slot on the top, no matter whether it is newspaper, message notes, or confidential documents.

A：That's no-brainer.

B：But before you insert the paper into the slot, you have to make sure there are not any metal things on the paper, for example, paper clips, because those kind of metal thing will destroy the cutter in the shredder.

A：I see. Then how long does it take for the shredder to cut a piece of paper.

B：Only several seconds. Finally, after the work is done, press the red button to switch it off.

A：What shall I do if the machine jams?

B：Don't worry. It's easy too. In case of machine jam, first of all, turn off the power. Do you remember how to turn off the power now?

A：Of course, just press the red button on its right side. Then what should I do next to solve the machine jam?

B：Then remove the jammed paper, and restart the machine.

A：I see. What if the motor overheats?

B：If it happens, then the machine switches off automatically. What you need to do is jut leave it for 15 – 30 minutes before the motor has cooled down and then you switch it on again.

A：Thank you so much! I have learnt a lot.

B：One more thing, don't put your fingers into the shredder, and be careful with long hair and loose clothing.

Dialogue 3 Office equipment problem solving and purchasing

Ken is working in a stationary company as a secretary. One day, her boss called her in and

asked her to solve the problem with his computer.

Boss: Hey, Jack, come to my office and have a look at my computer. I was not able to browse any web pages with it. What's up?

Ken: Em...let me see.

Ken: Seems that there are some network connectivity issues, I need some more time to identify the problem.

Boss: What nonsense! If network connectivity issues are related, how come you guys are able to?

Ken: Em...Boss, you know, the connection failure might be incurred by many factors, I do need time for troubleshooting...

Boss: No more excuse! Don't you think it is your own problem? Should the problem been caused by the computer, just bring me another one, else, I will find someone who can tell me what the problem is and how to solve it immediately.

(*Two days later, Ken is shopping in a computer shop.*)

Salesgirl: Hi, can I help you there?

Ken: No, I'm just looking. Thanks.

Salesgirl: Could I interest you in coming in to have a look at the wide range of computer equipment my company has to offer?

Ken: What sort of equipment?

Salesgirl: Everything from scanners to printers.

Ken: Do you have any Compaq Desktop with a price ranging from 4000 to 5000 RMB?

Salesgirl: Um, no. Sorry, only laptop are in stock now.

Ken: OK. Then do you have flat screen computer monitors?

Salesgirl: I am sorry. Only the normal variety.

Ken: What's the largest sized normal monitor you have?

Salesgirl: 21 inch.

Ken: Sorry, too small. I think I might just keep on looking.

Ⅳ. Practice

Practice 1　Translation

Translate the following passage about how to operate faxing machine into Chinese.

Faxing is an efficient way to quickly send documents that you don't have time to mail or the technology to scan. It is still the preferred method for sending signed documents. Fax machines can be confusing at first, however, using a personal fax machine does not have to be intimidating.

Step 1: Create a cover letter to use saying who the document is for and from as well as the intended fax number and your phone number. This alerts the office or home the fax is sent to who it is intended for. Place cover letter on top of your documents and insert them into the fax machine feeder facing in the direction the machine specifies.

_____

_____

Step 2: Enter the fax number into the machine. There will be a number pad just like a phone on the fax machine. Carefully type in the number so you do not make any mistakes, as it is difficult to know when you have dialed a wrong fax number.

_____

_____

Step 3: Hit the send key once you have properly entered all of the numbers into the machine. This will initiate the sending of the documents. The send key should be larger than the others and easy to locate. Traditionally, it is placed next to or below the keypad.

_____

_____

Step 4: Wait for your documents to pass through the machine and collect them when finished. Whatever you are sending will pass through a series of rollers that feed it through the machine and copy it digitally.

_____

_____

Step 5: Look for a confirmation page to print. This will tell you whether or not your fax successfully went through.

_____

_____

Practice 2　Word guessing

Work in groups. Each one thinks of 5 office equipment that are commonly used in modern offices. Then take turn to explain the 5 office equipment in your mind to other group members by describing their functions without mentioning their names. Then ask the other group members to guess what kind of office equipment you have described.

Practice 3　Debate

Nowadays, people do not write letters to their friends, business partners, or family members. Instead they send out an E-mail. Of course, E-mails are not good for everything. Debate in class with the topic: E-mail should totally replace letters.

Ⅴ. Course Project

In this project, Rachel and Robert will go through the last round of new employee training, that is office equipment, because as secretaries in a modern company, they are expected to be able to operate common office equipment. Therefore, today, their manager, Mr. Zhang will teach them how to operate the equipment in their office building.

Task 1

Mr. Zhang is telling what kind of equipment there are in their office building and what convenience those equipment bring to their work when showing them around the building. Suppose you are Mr. Zhang. Try explaining the functions of the following office equipment: computers, printers, fax machines, copiers, telephones, scanner, paper shredder, digital camera, typewriter, TV set, overhead projector. An example is given as below:

Fax machine—A machine which is used to instantly transmit information (letters, documents, pictures) via a telephone line to a destination fax machine.

Task 2

Your company, Great Stationary, just bought a paper shredder from DK Officemate Company. And Shown below is instructions for the machine. As a secretary with Great Stationary, you should be able to operate it, so you are asking Bill, the customer service engineer from DK, how to operate it. Try to role-play this situation on the basis of the instructions below, in which the customer service engineer is teaching the secretary how to operate the new machine.

Instructions

How to use
- *To switch on, press the green button.*
- *Put the paper in.*
- *To switch off, press the red button.*

Possible problems
- *The machine jams.*
- *The motor overheats.*

What to do
- *Press the red button. Remove the excess paper, then start again.*
- *The machine switches off automatically.*
- *Leave it for 15 – 30 minutes before you switch on again.*

Caution!
- *Do not put your fingers into the shredder.*
- *Be careful with long hair and loose clothing.*

Task 3

Your company, Great Stationary, is in need of a new printer. Your manager, Mr. Zhang, has asked you to purchase one. After searching the internet, you have two choices within your budget, whose ads are shown below. Discuss together with your partner to compare the advantages and disadvantages of the two printers, and decide which one to buy and provide your reasons.

☐ Compare

HP Officejet 6000 Wireless Printer

★★★☆☆ 3.3 out of 5
Read 13 reviews | Write a review

- Fast wired and wireless printing
- Professional color documents for lowest cost per page vs. in-class inkjets
- Cuts energy use by up to 40% compared with lasers
- Automatic two-sided printing

$89.99

3D VIEW

TM-T70 Receipt Printer

Get the high performance and reliability you need and streamline your POS system with Epson's space-saving TM-T70 thermal receipt printer. With its small size and low height(only 4.49″ high), it's designed to fit under your counter or in other small spaces, And all the features operate entirely from the front of the printer for easy access and easy maintenance.

$79.99

Product Features

- Front-facing controls, paper loading and receipt dispensing
- Small, space-saving footprint
- Designed to fit under counters
- Fast and versatile printing up to 170mm per second
- Sealed top for superior spill resistance
- Ease-of-use features including drop-in paper loading, autocutter and status LEDs
- Two-year warranty

TM-T70 Receipt Printer	
Interface	RS-232C, RS-485, Parallel, USB, Ethernet 10/100 Base TX, IEEE 802.11
Paper dimensions	3.13″±0.02″×3.27″diameter(79.5±0.5(W)×83.0mm)
Reliability	MTBF 360,000 hours MCBF 52,000,000 lines
Overall dimensions	4.92″(W)×7.64″(D)×4.49″(H);(125×194×114mm)
Case Color:	Epson Cool White, Epson Dark Gray

Project 6

On the Phone

Task 1　Picture recognition: tell the different kinds of telephone.

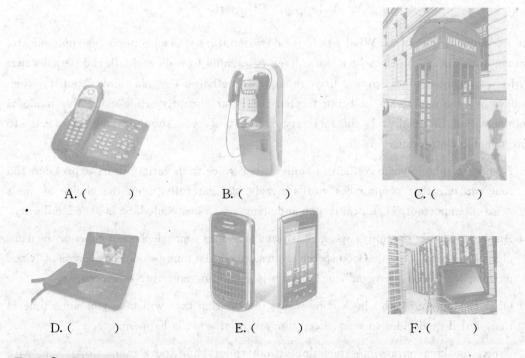

A. (　　　)　　　　　B. (　　　)　　　　　C. (　　　)

D. (　　　)　　　　　E. (　　　)　　　　　F. (　　　)

Task 2　Matching.

Match the English words and phrases with their Chinese counterparts.

1. message note　　　　　　a. 长途电话

2. handset　　　　　　　　b. 区号

3. answering machine　　　　c. 国际电话

4. dialing tone　　　　　　 d. 忙音

5. international call　　　　 e. 对方付费电话

6. long-distance call   f. 公用电话

7. information desk   g. 拨号音

8. screening   h. 免费电话

9. caller ID   i. 留言条

10. collect call/reverse-charge call   j. 查询台

11. engaged tone   k. 话机

12. telephone directory   l. 屏蔽电话号码

13. toll-free number   m. 留言机

14. area code   n. 电话号码本

15. pay phone/public phone   o. 来电显示

Ⅱ. Introduction to the Topic

Telephone Etiquette

The telephone is part of us. What would we do without it? It is as common as apple pie and summer sunshine. As much a part of our lives as learning to walk and talk and perhaps that is why we, at most times, give it little thought. Nonetheless, we do think about it, when we have had the experience of being treated rudely or abruptly while using this mode of communication. Especially, as the secretary or assistant, you should attach importance to more telephone etiquette.

(1) A good telephone voice contains a smile. It is a voice with variety in its expression and tone and one that pronounces words clearly and carefully. Even the choice of one's words is important. Technical jargon and slang are to be avoided. So is over-familiarity.

(2) Answer the phone promptly, speak clearly and announce your telephone number or the name of your company, or both. Good speech creates a good first impression. The addition of "Good morning" or "Good afternoon", or "Can I help you?" are more than ever necessary.

(3) Offer to ring your caller back if he wants information that will take you some time to find, but if he decides to wait, keep him aware of what is happening.

(4) When speaking on an imperfect line do not shout, but speak more slowly and with greater deliberation. Shouting causes distortion and makes matters worse.

(5) Be polite, but don't allow yourself to be brushed off. You have a right to information, especially from public agencies. If you've really tried to get help but are constantly meeting roadblocks, ask to speak to a supervisor.

(6) When the boss is not in the office, a secretary should be instructed to answer calls without saying where her boss is. The secretary should say, "Mr. Wang is out of the building on a business appointment", or something similar. It is the secretary's duty to

protect her boss from any possible criticism or misinterpretation of his whereabouts.

(7) One of the rudest and most aggravating occurrences in the everyday life is to have someone hang up when they call and find out it's wrong number. It is a common courtesy if one dials a wrong number to say, "I'm sorry", or "Please forgive me", before hanging up.

(8) The most important thing to remember about telephone manners is always to return one's calls promptly. Even if what one has to say is negative or unpleasant, he should make the call and get it over with.

For telephone message, the giver must state all the necessary information himself, without wasting the taker's time. He must enunciate his words, so that he is clearly understood. The message leaver should state:

- His name (full name)
- His company
- His telephone number
- His message, briefly stated and to the point

The message taker must write a full message down on a proper piece of paper, not the edge of an envelope or the back of another piece of paper. The person taking down the message should add the time the message was received.

Exercise: True or False

1. _____ When you speak to others in the phone call, you'd better laugh at them.
2. _____ If you need to find some information for a long time, please let the caller wait patiently.
3. _____ When the boss is not in, the secretary should tell the caller where he is honestly.
4. _____ When the line is not clear, you should shout at the caller and tell him to speak louder.
5. _____ When leaving message, the caller should tell the necessary information himself.

Ⅲ. Situational Dialogue

Dialogue 1　Making an appointment

Rachel:　Good afternoon, Great Stationery Co., Ltd.

Ms. Chen:　May I speak to Mr. Zhang, please?

Rachel:　Just a moment, I'll put you through.

Mr. Zhang: Speaking please.

Ms. Chen: Good afternoon, Mr. Zhang. My name is Chen Fang. Mr. Paul King asked me to phone you.

Mr. Zhang: Oh, good afternoon, Ms. Chen. Mr. Paul King said you'd ring.

Ms. Chen: Yes. He suggested we meet for dinner.

Mr. Zhang: Yes. What about Thursday the 15th, at the Swan Hotel at 6 p. m. ?

Mr. Chen: I'm afraid not. I have a presentation for that day. What about Friday afternoon?

Mr. Zhang: You bet! Expecting to meet you then.

Ms. Chen: See you then. Bye.

Dialogue 2   Leaving phone message

Mr. Paul King is phoning Mr. Zhang to ask something about their meeting next week, but unfortunately, Mr. Zhang's line is busy all the time. The following dialogue is between Mr. Paul King and Mr. Zhang's secretary Robert. A＝ Mr. Paul King, B＝ Robert.

A: Hello, could I speak to Mr. Zhang, please?

B: Who's calling please?

A: This is Mr. Paul King from Bridge Stationery Co. , Ltd.

B: Could you tell me what it's about, Mr. Paul King?

A: Yes, I'm calling about our meeting next week.

B: OK. Thank you. I'll put you through now.

(*After a pause.*)

B: The line is busy. Can I put you on hold?

A: Sure.

(*A few minutes later.*)

B: I'm afraid the line is still busy. Can I take a message for you, Mr. Paul King?

A: Yes, please. Could you tell him Mr. Paul King from Bridge Stationery Co. , Ltd. called and could you ask him to call me back?

B: Does he have your number, Mr. Paul King?

A: I think so, but I will give it to you again. It's 888-4560 extension 250.

B: So that's Mr. Paul King from Bridge Stationery Co. , Ltd. and your phone number is 888-4560, extension 250.

A: That's right.

B: I will get Mr. Zhang to call you back as soon as he is available.

A: Thank you. Goodbye.

B: You're welcome. Goodbye.

Dialogue 3   Making arrangement

Ms. Chen is phoning Mr. Zhang, the president of Great Stationery Co. , Ltd. to make an

appointment, and Rachel, Mr. Zhang's secretary answers the phone.

Rachel: Good morning, Great Stationery Co., Ltd. Mr. Zhang's office.

Chen: Hello, this is Chen Fang. I'm calling about the appointment with Mr. Zhang for this afternoon. Something's just come up, I'm afraid the appointment will have to be rescheduled. I'm very sorry about the change.

Rachel: That's all right. Maybe I can make another arrangement for you.

Chen: You're very kind to say so. Thank you. Do you think tomorrow morning would suit him?

Rachel: I'm afraid there's a bit of a problem. In fact, he's booked up the whole week except tomorrow afternoon.

Chen: Tomorrow afternoon? You see, I've made an appointment with Mr. Green for tomorrow afternoon. In order to meet Mr. Zhang, I'll have to cancel the appointment with Mr. Green, I'm afraid. Rachel: I'm terribly sorry, Sir, but Mr. Zhang is really busy this week.

Chen: I understand. When do you think I can come and see him tomorrow afternoon?

Rachel: Please let me check. Yes, he'll be free from 2:00 tomorrow afternoon. Do you think it's convenient for you?

Chen: Yes, that's quite all right for me. Thank you so much for your help.

Rachel: You are welcome. Thank you for calling.

IV. Practice

Practice 1   Leaving phone message

Student A: Ms. Chen wants to speak to Mr. Zhang about the contract with her company, Bridge Stationery Co., Ltd. If Mr. Zhang isn't in the office, leave the following information:

– Your name

– Telephone number

– Calling about your contract

– You can be reached until 5 o'clock at the above number

Student B: You are the secretary of Mr. Zhang. Ms. Chen would like to speak to Mr. Zhang, but he is out of the office. Take a message and make sure you get the following information:

– Name and telephone number—ask Ms. Chen to spell the surname.

– Message—Ms. Chen would like to leave for Mr. Zhang.

– How late Mr. Zhang can call Ms. Chen at the given telephone number.

You can use the format below to help you note down all the necessary information.

```
┌─────────────────────────────────────────────────────────────────┐
│                      Telephone message                          │
│   From：                          For：                          │
│   Time：                          Number：                       │
│   Message：                                                      │
│                                                                 │
│                                                                 │
│                                                                 │
└─────────────────────────────────────────────────────────────────┘
```

Practice 2　Making an appointment

Student A：You are a secretary from Bridge Stationery Co. , Ltd. Your boss wants you to phone Great Stationery Co. , Ltd. to make an appointment with Mr. Zhang for an informal meeting next Monday.

Student B：You are a secretary. Mr. Zhang is away on business today. You are supposed to fix schedule for Mr. Zhang for next week. Mr. Zhang will be available at 9：00 a. m. next Monday.

Practice 3　Making telephone call

Student A：You are the secretary working at Mr. Zhang's office. You ask Mr. Paul King to hold on, and help put him through.

Student B：You are the customer Mr. Paul King. You are from England. You want to speak to Mr. Zhang.

Ⅴ.Course Project

In the previous units, Rachel and Robert have gone through new employee training in which they have understood their job duties and etiquette as secretaries, familiarized themselves with their office environment, learned how to use office equipment. Now they are ready to start their work. Today, they have several telephone calls to make and several telephone calls to answer.

Task 1

Ms. Chen, the sales representative of your supplier, Bridge Stationery Co. , Ltd. calls your boss' office, wanting to discuss the price change of plastic packages. Your boss is out for lunch, you are expected to explain it to Ms. Chen, and take her message and fill out the message note below.

```
┌─────────────────────────────────────────────────────┐
│                  TELEPHONE MESSAGE                    │
│  To Mr. / Miss / Mrs. _____ │
│  From Mr. / Miss / Mrs. _____ │
│  Of _____│
│  Tel No. _____│
│  Date _____     Time _____          │
│                                                       │
│  Please call back (  )  Will call again (  )  Urgent ( )│
│  Message: _____│
│  _____ │
│  _____ │
│  _____ │
│                                                       │
│  Received by _____                                  │
└─────────────────────────────────────────────────────┘
```

Task 2

One of the company's clients, Mr. Paul King, the CEO of Bridge Stationery Co. , Ltd. calls with the hope of making an appointment with your boss, Mr. Zhang, to discuss their orders for next season. But Mr. Zhang is not in his office, you are expected to answer the phone, and make an appointment for your boss and Mr. Paul King.

Task 3

Mr. Zhang is the boss of Great Stationery Co. , Ltd. . Here is his schedule for the coming week.

May	7th	8th	9th	10th
A. M.	8:30－11:00 regular meeting	－12:00 business trip	10:00－11:30 factory tour	10:30－11:00 ceremony
P. M.	1:00－ business trip to Shanghai	3:00－4:30 meeting with Mr. Zhao	1:30－3:00 general meeting	have a rest

Suppose you are Mr. Zhang's secretary. You get a phone call from Mr. Paul King, a business partner of your company. He wants to make an appointment to see Mr. Zhang. Please arrange an appointment for him according to Mr. Zhang's schedule.

Project 7

Instruction and Request

Task 1　Picture recognition. What are they talking about for inquiring? Can you act it out with your partner?

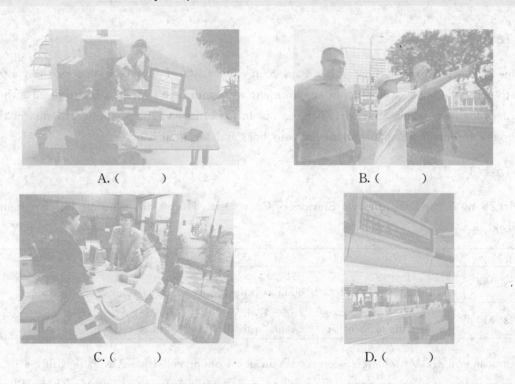

A. (　　)

B. (　　)

C. (　　)

D. (　　)

Task 2　Matching.

Match the English words and phrases with their Chinese counterparts.

1. ask for instructions　　　　a. 分配，委派
2. be entitled to　　　　　　　b. 弹性工作制
3. assignment　　　　　　　　c. 陪着，伴随
4. emphasis　　　　　　　　　d. 创新的，革新的

5. dictation　　　　　　　　　　　e. 请示

6. flexitime　　　　　　　　　　　f. 严厉,严格执行

7. indication　　　　　　　　　　 g. 强调,侧重点

8. persuasive　　　　　　　　　　 h. 具体的,明确的

9. rigor　　　　　　　　　　　　 i. 指示

10. accompany　　　　　　　　　　j. 部下,下属

11. specific　　　　　　　　　　　k. 口述

12. transaction　　　　　　　　　 l. 被给予……权利(做某事)

13. innovative　　　　　　　　　　m. 稳健的,缓和的

14. subordinate　　　　　　　　　 n. 有说服力的

15. moderate　　　　　　　　　　 o. 办理,处理,执行

Ⅱ. Introduction to the Topic

Getting Along with Your Boss and Colleagues

An important element of a secretary's success lies in their skills in dealing with people. In order to work happily and effectively in a company, a secretary should keep a good relationship with their boss and colleagues.

As for getting along with the boss, the secret is to adapt. A successful secretary must be familiar with the boss and understand the boss. First, a secretary should know the boss' character and habits well. If the boss is used to having a cup of coffee before starting the work, he would expect one on the table on coming into the office every morning. Second, a secretary should know much about the thinking mode, working style and social contacts of the boss, and this, to some extent, will make their work much easier. Only when the secretary knows all these, can they properly deal with something that may happen suddenly.

The following story will give you more hints.

Alice is a secretary in Mr. Baker's company. They have a very good relationship. She knows how to deal with her boss when he makes a mistake. She also knows she shouldn't say "You are wrong!", but uses an indirect approach.

Just last week, Mr. Baker was talking to Alice about a TCL contract. Mr. Baker wasn't very familiar with the terms. He forgot the deadline and thought the delivery date was in June instead of May. But Alice skillfully reminded him by asking questions which began with the questions: "Isn't it…" and "Didn't we…" as if she herself wasn't really sure. This made it easier for Mr. Baker to accept the correction.

When Mr. Baker made a mistake about the discount, this time Alice used the words, "Actually…", and "I believe…" to make an indirect correction. She also showed Mr. Baker the meeting minutes as a proof.

In the end Mr. Baker decided to stick to the original deadline instead of pushing it forward.

On the other hand, good relationships with colleagues are also very important. A secretary should respect others by listening to them and trying to understand them. Though the colleagues have different backgrounds and interests, the secretary needs to accept them without prejudice, and learn more about them to avoid conflicts that result from a lack of understanding. Moreover, the secretary should be willing to cooperate. Since much work can't be performed alone, team spirit becomes more important.

In one word, warmth, friendliness, honesty and credibility are the core of a secretary's manner. ①

Exercise：True or False

1. _____ The secretary should make some changes in order to get along with the boss.

2. _____ An excellent secretary should prepare everything for the boss.

3. _____ As a secretary, you'd better listen to your boss and not quarrel with him.

4. _____ The story tells us that the boss is not always right, as an assistant, you can communicate with him rationally.

5. _____ To get along with your boss and colleagues, you should be polite, skillful and considerate.

Ⅲ. Situational Dialogue

Dialogue 1   Instruction about the fax

Zhang： Rachel, have you received the fax from Bridge Stationery Co. ?

Rachel： No, sir. I have called Ms. Chen and she told me that their fax machine was out of order and she would send us the fax later.

(*20 minutes later.*)

Rachel： I have received the fax from Bridge Stationery Co. . Here it is, sir.

Zhang： Oh, that is terrible. The fax has been muddled. What's worse, page four is missing. Would you please ask them to send us the fax again?

Rachel： All right, sir.

(*Rachel then calls Ms. Chen.*)

Rachel： Hello. This is Rachel. May I speak to Ms. Chen, please?

Chen： This is Chen Fang.

Rachel： Ms. Chen, would you please send me the fax again? The fax you sent me just now

---

① 蔡昕. 文秘英语. 北京:外语教学与研究出版社,2007

was very not clear and page four is missing.

Chen: I am sorry. I will send you the fax again right now.

Rachel: Thank you so such.

Chen: You are welcome.

Dialogue 2　Discussion on the schedule

Rachel: Mr. Zhang, I've drafted a schedule for your business trip next week. You may have a look. You can make some changes if it does not suit you.

Zhang: Oh, great! Let's discuss it together. Now, when am I off then?

Rachel: You are leaving on Tuesday morning.

Zhang: What time exactly?

Rachel: Your flight takes off at 8:10 a. m. And you arrive in Shanghai at 10:40. Mr. Yang is meeting you at the airport.

Zhang: I see. What about activities?

Rachel: You are attending the conference on Wednesday morning and in the afternoon you are going to the exhibition. On Thursday, you are inspecting the factory in the morning and having dinner with him in the evening.

Zhang: I've got a schedule. How about the appointment with Mr. Wang?

Rachel: Shall I postpone it until you're back?

Zhang: Very good! Thank you for your arrangement.

Dialogue 3　Making assignment

Rachel: Hello, Mr. Zhang. What do you want me to do?

Zhang: Hello, Rachel. Can you send the plans to me before Friday?

Rachel: All right, Mr. Zhang. I'll get those plans over to your office by Friday morning.

Zhang: Great. That will give me time to talk with my partner before I make a final decision.

Rachel: That's what I want. I'll have them there by Friday.

Zhang: Thank you. By the way, I need you to write a letter, deliver this package and call my lawyer.

Rachel: Yes, sir. Which would you like me to do first?

Zhang: Please deliver the package first since it is the most urgent. Then call my lawyer, and then I'll be ready to dictate my letter.

Rachel: OK, sir. I will be back soon.

Zhang: Wait! Sorry, I forget this. Could you ask Robert to copy this document for me?

Rachel: How many copies would you want?

Zhang: Fifty.

Rachel: Yes, sir. Will there be anything else?

Zhang: No, thank you. That will be all for now.

IV. Practice

Practice 1　Instruction on writing E-mail

Student A: You are Mr. Zhang, the boss of Great Stationery Co., Ltd. A meeting will be held next Monday. You want your assistant Rachel to write an E-mail and send it to relevant participants.

Student B: You are Rachel. You inquire some information about the meeting, for example, the topic, the place, the participants, etc. and take them down.

Practice 2　Discussion on making appointment

Student A: You are the boss, Mr. Zhang. Recently you want to establish business relationship with another company, Officemate Trading Co., Ltd. You ask your secretary to make a phone call and make an appointment talking face to face.

Student B: You are the secretary of the company. You have a discussion with your boss about it.

Practice 3　Talking about contract

Student A: You are Mr. Zhang, a manager.

Student B: You are Rachel, a secretary.

> Notes:
> Bridge Stationery
>   – contact Ms. Chen
>   – ordered 5 office suites
>   – 12% discount (originally 17%)
>   – delivery in 6 days

Try to make a conversation according to the notes made by Rachel about a contact with Bridge Stationery.

V. Course Project

How do you deal with your boss when he is in a rush? The secret is to ask the right questions in the right way. What do you do if your boss makes some mistakes? You must not say, "You are wrong!" A better way is to use an indirect approach and remind him by asking questions such as, "Isn't it...?" or "Didn't we..."

Task 1

Rachel works for Mr. Zhang, a businessman, as his secretary. The company will extend other business fields and needs more employees. Mr. Zhang calls Rachel into his office and give her some instructions.

Task 2

The end of the year is coming. By rule, a party will be held. Mr. Yang, the office dean, asks the assistants from some departments to discuss the relevant details. They are asking for and giving instructions.

Task 3

You are a secretary and new to the company, ask for instructions of the daily routine work. Robert is the assistant of the manager, he tells you what you should do and what you shouldn't do.

Project 8
At a Meeting

Task 1 Picture recognition. Can you tell the role they play in the meeting?

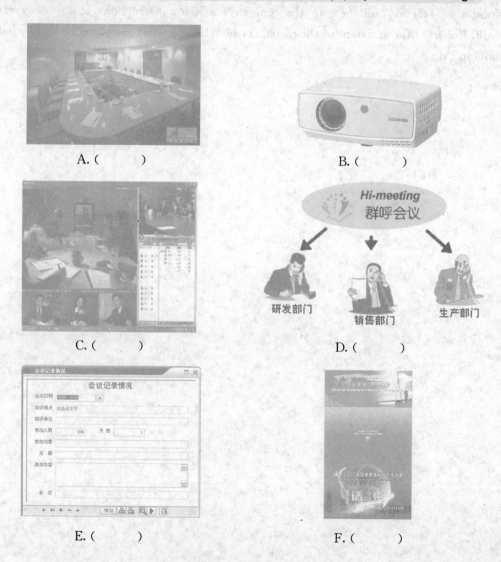

A. (   )

B. (   )

C. (   )

D. (   )

E. (   )

F. (   )

Task 2   Matching.

Match the English words and phrases with their Chinese counterparts.

1. notice board
2. Executive Committee
3. working paper
4. declaration/statement
5. make a speech/deliver a speech
6. proposal
7. raise an objection
8. summary record
9. resolution
10. support
11. comment
12. Standing Committee
13. first draft/preliminary draft
14. procedure
15. oppose

a. 做报告
b. 建议
c. 布告牌
d. 提出异议
e. 摘要记录
f. 执行委员会
g. 决议
h. 声明
i. 赞成
j. 工作文件
k. 常务委员会
l. 程序
m. 反对
n. 评论
o. 草案、初稿

Ⅱ. Introduction to the Topic

Making Meetings More Productive

Many managers and workers complain about unproductive meetings. White-collar workers spend on average one to one and a half days each week in meetings, according to a survey last year. Many managers spend as much as 33 hours a week in conferences. And meetings are increasing as more employees work in teams.

How do you ensure that your meetings are productive? First, decide whether a meeting is really necessary. If you just need to give information to workers, it's better to use E-mail or a memo. It's also a lot cheaper than pulling employees away from work. Second, invite only those who really need to attend. The most productive meetings are those done in small groups of four or five. Small meetings tend to be more focused than large ones. They also force participants to be prepared. Third, the agenda is also necessary. Most meetings have an agenda. For a formal meeting, this document is usually circulated in advance to all participants. For an informal meeting, the agenda may be simply a list of the points that have to be dealt with.

Lack of preparation is one of the top complaints about meetings. As the chairman, remember to start the meeting on time, and don't let it run on too long.

If you are the presenter, a well-planned presentation will make you look good. Here are some guidelines:

Remember your listeners' needs. How long will people be sitting? You may decide to stop and take a break in the presentation at a mid-point.

Develop outlines. For each section of the presentation, identify key points to make.

Focus on clarity. In general, simpler is better.

Use visuals. Visuals add variety to a presentation. But don't use too many, and avoid turning down the lights for too long, especially after lunch.

Plan to arrive early and check your equipment. Make sure that video screens and projectors are well-placed and working.

Furthermore, videoconferencing, as business tool, appeared increasingly in more and more small business meetings. Apart from reducing travel, videoconferencing systems have other useful features. For example, using a function called a shared whiteboard, participants at great distances can work on the same document at the same time, or see the results instantly on their computer screens. The technology lets us see each other's face and hand gestures, which gives us much better communication than we would have just talking on the phone.

In order to go through the meeting procedure smoothly, we, chairperson or participants, should obeys the rules, and keep harmony with your group.

Last but not least, offer a summary of what has been accomplished at the meeting. Ask if there is any uncertainty about the action items. Inquire about new items of business for consideration for the next meeting. Announce the time and date of the next meeting. Be sure to thank the group members for their time and contributions. And finally, officially adjourn the meeting.

Exercise: True or False

1. _____ Meetings should be held regularly for each week.
2. _____ For a small-sized meeting, the agenda is not necessary.
3. _____ For an effective meeting, it should have the clear resolution finally.
4. _____ In order to make the meeting productive, preparation is of vital importance.
5. _____ The participants can disturb the spokesman and express their ideas at any moment.

Ⅲ. Situational Dialogue

Dialogue 1　Checking the preparation for the meeting

Rachel, an experienced and proficient secretary, is asking Robert, a junior secretary, if

everything is ready for the meeting.

Rachel: Is the room ready for the meeting, Robert?

Robert: Yes, I've put the minute book and some paper copies of the agenda on the table. And paper and pencils have been laid next to their name cards of each attendant.

Rachel: Thank you. How about the microphone and speakers?

Robert: I also have got them ready for the meeting.

Rachel: Good, I've come to tell you that you'll have to take down the minutes this afternoon.

Robert: Should I write down every word people say?

Rachel: No, you needn't do that. That's very difficult and hardly ever necessary. You just make a note of the topics that are discussed and the result of the discussion.

Robert: And should I type out the minutes from the notes?

Rachel: Yes, of course.

Dialogue 2   Reporting to the boss

Zhang: Rachel, would you please come in for a while? Please also bring along the minutes of yesterday's management meeting.

Rachel: Of course, Sir... Here is the minutes of the meeting.

Zhang: How long did the meeting last?

Rachel: The meeting was delayed by thirty minutes and it lasted for two and a half hours.

Zhang: Did the chairman ask for me?

Rachel: Yes, I told him that you were very ill and couldn't attend.

Zhang: All right. Have you handed in my report to him?

Rachel: Yes, I did. Besides, here are all the reports and materials handed out in the meeting. I think you'll have to do some replies.

Zhang: Thank you, Rachel. You've done an excellent job. Did they mention the date for the next meeting?

Rachel: No, they didn't. The chairman said he would send a memo to all managers by the end of this week informing them of the date of the next meeting.

Dialogue 3   Having a meeting on advertisement

Zhang: Let's talk about how we're going to advertise our new stereo systems. The market is teenagers and young adults. What approaches could we use to appeal to that market?

Rachel: Well, I think we really need to get our brand name out there. We could increase visibility with TV commercials.

Zhang: Yes, but it's too expensive. If we bought TV air time, we could be well over budget.

Rachel: OK. What about radio advertising? That's cheaper.

Zhang: Yes. Radio advertising might work if we placed the ads well. But that would also be too expensive given our budget.

Robert: What if we advertised on billboards?

Rachel: I don't think highway signs would be appropriate. But I think billboards could work if we focused on subway and train advertising.

Robert: How about advertising on the Web?

Zhang: Well, advertising on the Web would reach a lot of young people. That's a good idea.

Rachel: I agree. Taking the budget into consideration, it is the most cost-effective.

Ⅳ. Practice

Practice 1   Meeting information

Student A: You are Rachel, the secretary of Great Stationery Co., Ltd. Call one of your important customers Ms. Chen, in order to tell her to participate in an urgent meeting. Include the place, the time, etc.

Student B: You are Ms. Chen. You take down the points that Rachel said. Inquire the topic of the meeting and preparation needed.

Practice 2   Chat before the meeting

Student A: You are Ms. Chen, the sales representative from Bridge Stationery Co. You arrived at the meeting hall in advance and sat on the sofa reading magazines.

Student B: You are Rachel, the assistant of Mr. Zhang. Now you've finished preparation needed for the meeting. So walked forward to Ms. Chen, and had an active discussion with her.

Practice 3   Preparation for the meeting

Student A: You are Robert. You worked as a secretary only for two weeks. Your company will hold a meeting after a week. So you are going to ask Rachel who worked here for about 3 years.

Student B: You are Rachel, the assistant of the manager, tell the new employee about preparation before the meeting.

Ⅴ. Course Project

In the previous unit, you've learned how to deal with your boss. As a sectary, you should listen to your boss and obey what he said. For example, before the meeting is held, you'd better ask for instructions, then make preparation according to your boss' idea.

Task 1

There will be a trade fair next month. Your company is one of the organizers. One day, you go to the manager's office asking for instructions about the fair. Your manager tells you what you should prepare for. You take down the points and inquire some details.

Task 2

Many employees complain about the tedious and frequent meetings. Rachel, Mr. Zhang's assistant, made a report to him. They discuss the reasons and put forward some suggestive points for a productive meeting.

Task 3

Recently, sales quota went down sharply. Paul King asks his secretary, Ms. Chen to notify all the department directors to have a meeting. At the meeting, they express their ideas and discuss the strategies on how to turn the situation in the near future.

Project 9

E-mail

Task 1   Recognition.

There are different styles of E-mail. After reading the following E-mails, decide which style each belong to.

Fm: (support@surveys.com)

Date: 2010年2月19日2:02:05

To: xxx@hotmail.com

Dear member,

I work as part of a news research team and I'm currently working on a project to find out more about our audience's travel habits. I'd really like to know more about things like the number of flights you take every year, where you'd like to go on holiday, and what sort of activities you like to try.

This survey should only take around 10 minutes. Your answers will help me build a picture of our audience's interests and experiences and will be used by different teams within the news company. Please click here to start the survey. The survey will be open until Saturday 27th February.

Click here to start the survey.

Thanks.

Kima

(blocked style E-mail)

Subject: http://mikesdomain.org

From: "Vanessa Lintner" reply@seekercenter.net

Reply-To: "Vanessa Lintner" vanessa@seekercenter.net

To: webmaster@mikesdomain.org

　I have visited mikesdomain.org and noticed that your website is not listed on some search engines.

I am sure that through our service the number of people who visit your website will definitely increase. SeekerCenter is a unique technology that instantly submits your website to over 500,000 search engines and directories-a really low-cost and effective way to advertise your site. For more details please go to www. SeekerCenter. net. Give your website maximum exposure today. Looking forward to hearing from you.

Best Regards, Vanessa Lintner Sales & Marketing

Source: http://www. michaelhorowitz. com/badE-mails. html

(indented style E-mail)

Task 2   Matching.

Match the English words and phrases with their Chinese counterparts.

1. E-mail   a. 网址
2. Website address   b. 网民
3. Internet user   c. 电子邮件
4. Bandwidth   d. 带宽
5. Coverage   e. 发送者
6. Sender   f. 网络安全
7. Receiver   g. 协议
8. Protocol   h. 覆盖范围
9. Firewall   i. 接收者
10. Online security   j. 防火墙
11. Hacker   k. 病毒
12. Virus   l. 黑客
13. Online security   m. 网络安全
14. Anti-virus software   n. 防病毒软件
15. Junk mail   o. 垃圾邮件

Ⅱ. Introduction to the Topic

Electronic mail, or E-mail for short, is an entirely new way of communication by means of computers. Being fast, inexpensive, highly efficient and convenient, E-mail is so popular in both developed and developing countries that it is difficult to imagine modern life without it.

Nowadays, millions of computers all over the world have been connected to form a global network called Internet. You can send or receive by E-mail a variety of information and documents such as letters, papers, video and audio files to anyone in over 170 countries in a short time. Moreover, language barriers are not a problem, because Internet software is capable of translating your E-mail into whatever language you want. You can also store, delete, edit, compile and search your E-mail. Most importantly, E-mail helps us overcome space and time limitations in communication. ①

With the rapidly growing popularity of computers and the fast expansion of the information highway, wider and wider applications of Internet E-mail will be developed and E-mail will soon become an indispensable means of communication.

Important Points to Remember

–E-mail is much less formal than a written letter. E-mails are usually short and concise.

–If you are writing to someone you don't know, a simple "Hello" is adequate. Using a salutation such as "Dear Mr. Smith," is too formal.

–When writing to someone you know well, feel free to write as if you are speaking to the person.

– Use abbreviated verb forms (He's, We're, He'd, etc.)

–Include a telephone number to the signature of the E-mail. This will give the recipient the chance to telephone if necessary.

–It is not necessary to include your E-mail address as the recipient can just reply to the E-mail.

–When replying eliminate all the information that is not necessary. Only leave the sections of text that are related to your reply. This will save your readers' time when reading your E-mail. ②

E-mail format:

To: type the E-mail address where the message is going.

Cc: type other E-mail addresses to which the message will be sent.

Sub or Re: type a brief description of the content.

Exercise: True or False

1. _____E-mails are popular and efficient but expensive.

2. _____E-mails can be translated into any language you need.

3. _____ We can correct our E-mails if we find wrong spellings.

4. _____ Always address the recipient with "Dear Mr. A".

5. _____ We should keep an E-mail as concise as possible.

---

① www. zlcool. com/zw/5/.../c7c22d485e67c1ae8525f1c276c20413. html,2010-12-30

② http://esl. about. com/od/businessenglishwriting/a/bizdocs_3. htm,2010-12-30

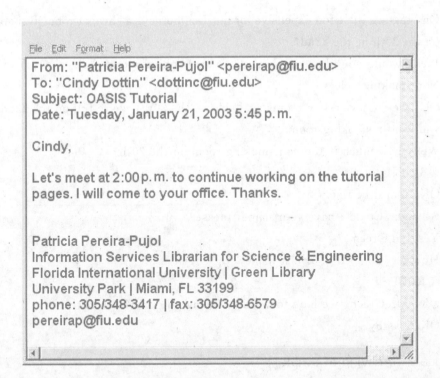

File Edit Format Help

From: "Patricia Pereira-Pujol" <pereirap@fiu.edu>
To: "Cindy Dottin" <dottinc@fiu.edu>
Subject: OASIS Tutorial
Date: Tuesday, January 21, 2003 5:45 p.m.

Cindy,

Let's meet at 2:00 p.m. to continue working on the tutorial
pages. I will come to your office. Thanks.

Patricia Pereira-Pujol
Information Services Librarian for Science & Engineering
Florida International University | Green Library
University Park | Miami, FL 33199
phone: 305/348-3417 | fax: 305/348-6579
pereirap@fiu.edu

Ⅲ. Situational Dialogue

Dialogue 1 Booking through E-mails

Mr. Green called to see if he can book a room through E-mails. The following dialogue is between Mr. Green and Hotel clerk.

Clerk: Hello. Holiday Inn. May I help you?

Green: Yes, first I'd like to know if I could book a room through your website or E-mails.

Clerk: Our E-mail system is updating. Next month, it'll work.

Green: I see. Then I'd like to reserve a room for two on the 21st of March.

Clerk: OK. Let me check our books here for a moment. The 21st of May, right?

Green: No. March, not May.

Clerk: Oh, sorry. Let me see here. Hmmm.

Green: Are you all booked that night?

Clerk: Well, we do have one suite available, with a sauna bath. And the view of the sea is great, too.

Green: How much is that?

Clerk: It's only $200 dollars.

Green: Oh, that's a little too expensive for me. Do you have a cheaper room available either on the 20th or the 22nd?

Clerk: Well, would you like a smoking or a non-smoking room?

Green: Non-smoking, please.

Clerk: OK, we do have a few rooms available on the 20th; we're full on the 22nd, unless you want a smoking room.

Green: Well, how much is the non-smoking room on the 20th?

Clerk: $ 80 dollars.

Green: OK, that'll be fine.

Clerk: All right. Could I have your name, please?

Green: Yes. Jim Green.

Clerk: How do you spell your last name, Mr. Green?

Green: G-R-E-E-N.

Clerk: OK, Mr. Green, we look forward to seeing you on March 20th.

Green: OK. Goodbye.

Dialogue 2   Arriving at a hotcl

Mr. Green arrived at the hotel.

Clerk: Good morning, Sir.

Green: Good morning, my name is Green. I called you a couple of days ago to make a reservation.

Clerk: Oh, yes, Mr. Green, a double room with sauna bath.

Green: That's me.

Clerk: And you have booked two nights.

Green: That's right.

Clerk: Here's your key, Mr. Green. Room 504. It's on the fifth floor. There's a lift on your right. Have a nice evening.

Green: Thank you.

Dialogue 3   Checking out of a hotel

Clerk: Good morning. May I help you?

Green: Yes, I'd like to check out now. My name is Green, room 504. Here is the key.

Clerk: One moment, please, Sir. Here's your bill. Would you like to check and see if the amount is correct?

Green: What's the 17 dollars for?

Clerk: That's for the phone calls you made from your room.

Green: Can I pay with ID card?

Clerk: Certainly. May I have your passport, please?

Green: Here you are.

Clerk: Could you sign your name here for me?

Green: Sure.

Clerk: Here is your receipt, sir. Thank you.

Green: Thank you. Goodbye.

Ⅳ. Practice

Practice 1

Tom Green, president of ABC company, is not available on March 2nd, 2010 (Tuesday) for an appointment with Mr. Zhang, president of Textile Import and Export Company. The appointment has to be rescheduled. Now Jack, secretary to Mr. Green, is writing an E-mail to Mr. Zhang to reset another date for the meeting.

Ss E-mail

> Fm: tomgreen@abc.com
> To: zhang@tiec.com
> Date: Thursday, February 25, 2010
> Subject: not available on Tuesday afternoon
>
> Dear Mr. Zhang,
> I'm writing to inform you that because I have something else to do I can't meet you on Tuesday after-noon. You know, there's something that needs to be taken care of so I am sorry that I can't meet you on Tuesday afternoon. Can we meet another time?
> Let me know.
>
> Tom Green
> President of ABC company
> tomgreen@abc.com

Ss discuss on the E-mail and form their opinions on how to write a good E-mail.

Practice 2

After receiving the E-mail from Mr. Green, Mr. Zhang's secretary checks his schedule and writes an E-mail to propose 2 p. m. Wednesday (March 3rd) for the appointment since Mr. Zhang will be occupied all week except on that afternoon.

Ss' E-mail

Fm: zhang@tiec.com
To: tomgreen@abc.com
Date: Thursday, February 25, 2010
Subject: available on Wednesday afternoon

Dear Mr. Green,

Your E-mail earlier today mentioned the change in your schedule. Since you have something urgent to deal with, then let's put it on Wednesday afternoon, say at 2 pm. If that's OK with you, please let me know asap.
Thanks.

Mr. Zhang
President of Textile Import and Export Company
zhang@tiec.com

Ss discuss on the E-mail and form their opinions on how to write a good E-mail.

Practice 3

A financial crisis hits in and ABC Company needs to make better budgets and cuts down costs. Mr. Green wants all department managers to think of ways to reduce running expenditures in each department and report to him on Tuesday morning. His secretary is preparing the E-mail.

Ss' E-mail

Fm: tomgreen@abc.com
To: finance@abc.com, sales@abc.com, hr@abc.com, administration@abc.com
Date: Thursday, February 25, 2010
Subject: Cutting down costs

All department managers,
I'm writing to inform you that the financial crisis hits in and ABC company needs to make better budgets and cuts down costs. I want all department managers to think of ways to reduce running expenditures in each department and report to him on Tuesday morning.
Let me know.

Tom Green
President of ABC company
tomgreen@abc.com

Ss form in groups and discuss on the E-mail.

V. Course Project

Task 1

Miss Chen, the sales representative of your supplier, Bridge Stationery Co., calls your boss' office, wanting to know the reason for the price increase of plastic packages. On behalf of your boss, you are expected to send an E-mail and explain it.

Task 2

One of the company's clients, Mr. Fang, the purchasing manager of Eco-Office Trading Co., complains of a late delivery of the goods. You're expected to send a reply and explain why the delivery was late and offer compensation for it if necessary.

Task 3

Mr. Paul King, the CEO of Officemate Trading Co. Ltd., one of leading stationery importers in U.K., is visiting your company on November 23. You, as the secretary, are asked to book a hotel room for him. According to your company's policy and Mr. King's position, you should book a suite in a five-star hotel, with a price of around 1000 RMB per night. After booking the room, you're expected to write an E-mail to Mr. Paul King and inform him of all the details.

Project 10

Memos

Task 1　Recognition.

There are different ways of communication and correspondence. After reading the following texts, decide which way of communication each belong to.

----- Message from &#0067itiba&#0110k <AurelieHarriett service_center@citicards.com> on Wed 18 Aug 2004 04:17:51 +0000 -----

To:	test@yahoo.com
Subject:	C&#0105&#0116&#0105&#0098&#0097n&#0107 email ver ification - test@yahoo.com

Dear Citibank Member,

This E-mail was sent by the Citibank server to verify your E-mail address.　You must complete this process by clicking on the link below and entering in the small window your Citibank ATM/Debit Card number and PIN that you use on ATM. This is done for your protection—because some of ourmembers no longer have access to their E-mail addresses and we must verify it.

To verify your E-mail address and access your bank account, click on the link below:

www.citibank.com/?q9HlxPDzLmleRmE2MKm837o8xe5n3lt8lD0jT3xXhjBel1399oEkp988b6k

---

（**E-mail**）

Task 2　Matching.

Match the English words and phrases with their Chinese counterparts.

1. memorandum
2. format

a. 障碍
b. 缩略的

WALT DISNEY PRODUCTIONS, *Ltd.*

INTER-OFFICE COMMUNICATION

TO MR __All personnel IBT Dept.__　　　DATE __January 17 1939__

FROM MR __Hal Adelquist__　　　SUBJECT __Departmental conduct__

Attention has been called to the rather gross language that is being used by some members of the IBT Department in the presence of some of our female employees.

It has always been Walt's hope that the Studio could be a place where girls can be employed without fear of embarassment or humiliation.

Your cooperation in this matter will be appreciated.

（memo）

Post Office, San Francisco, Calif.

August 4, 1926.

UNDER a recent ruling of the Post Office Department, letters mailed at ship's side will be charged with double the usual rates of postage when handed to representatives of the post office at the port of dispatch.

Letters may also be handed to sea post clerks of vessels carrying sea post offices, in which case only the usual postage will be required.

JAMES E. POWER.

Postmaster.

2232—San Francisco P. O. 8-19-26—5000.

（notice）

3. barrier　　　　　　　　c. 备忘录

4. software　　　　　　　d. 称呼，称谓

5. compile　　　　　　　e. 信息高速公路

6. information highway　　f. 编辑整理

7. indispensable　　　　　g. 不可或缺的

8. salutation　　　　　　h. 接受者，收信人

9. abbreviated	i. 格式
10. recipient	j. 软件
11. Office document	k. 简明的
12. Concise	l. 操作简单的
13. User-friendly	m. 办公室文件
14. Effective message	n. 双向交流
15. Two-way communication	o. 有效的信息

Ⅱ. Introduction to the Topic

Memos

A memorandum or memo is a document or other communication that aids the memory by recording events or observations on a topic, such as may be used in a business office. The plural form is either memoranda or memorandums.

A memorandum may have any format, or it may have a format specific to an office or institution. In law specifically, a memorandum is a record of the terms of a transaction or contract, such as a policy memo, memorandum of understanding, memorandum of agreement, or memorandum of association. Alternative formats include memos, briefing notes, reports, letters or binders. They could be one page long or many. If the user is a cabinet minister or a senior executive, the format might be rigidly defined and limited to one or two pages. If the user is a colleague, the format is usually much more flexible. At its most basic level, a memorandum can be a handwritten note to one's supervisor. [①]

Memos have a twofold purpose: they bring attention to problems and they solve problems. They accomplish their goals by informing the reader about new information like policy changes, price increases, or by persuading the reader to take an action, such as attend a meeting, or change a current production procedure. Regardless of the specific goal, memos are most effective when they connect the purpose of the writer with the interests and needs of the reader.

Choose the audience of the memo wisely. Ensure that all of the people that the memo is addressed to need to read the memo. If it is an issue involving only one person, do not send the memo to the entire office. Also, be certain that material is not too sensitive to put in a memo; sometimes the best forms of communication are face-to-face interaction or a phone call. Memos are most effectively used when sent to a small to moderate amount of people to

---

① http://en.wikipedia.org/wiki/Memorandum, 2010-12-30

communicate company or job objectives. ①

Important Points to Remember

Use the following structure to begin a memo.

MEMO

From: (person or group sending the memo)

To: (person or group to whom the memo is addressed)

RE: (the subject of the memo, this should be in bold)

- The term "memorandum" can be used instead of "memo".

- A memo is generally not as formal as a written letter. However, it is certainly not as informal as a personal letter.

- The tone of a memo is generally friendly as it is a communication between colleagues.

- Keep the memo concise and to the point.

- If necessary, introduce the reason for the memo with a short paragraph.

- Use bullet points to explain the most important steps in a process.

- Use a short thank you to finish the memo. This need not be as formal as in a written letter.

Exercise: True or False

1. _____ The format of a memorandum is quite restricted.

2. _____ A memo can be as simple as a manually-written note to one's boss.

3. _____ A memo needs to clarify why and to whom it is written.

4. _____ A memo is most effective when delivered to a small group of people.

5. _____ A memo should be as formal as possible.

Ⅲ. Situational Dialogue

Dialogue 1   Purpose of memos

Rachel is talking to Leslie, an intern on memos.

Leslie: Rachel, what's the difference between a memo and a business letter?

Rachel: Well, a memo is a document typically used for communication within a company. The heading and overall tone make a memo different from a business letter.

Leslie: So you're saying a business letter is more formal than a memo?

Rachel: Right. Since you generally send memos to co-workers and colleagues, you do not have to include a formal salutation or closing remark.

---

① http://owl.english.purdue.edu/owl/resource/590/01/, 2010-12-31

Leslie: What do co-workers and colleagues communicate in memos?

Rachel: Most memos communicate basic information, such as meeting times or due dates. But we might also write a memo to persuade others to take action, give feedback on an issue, or react to a situation.

Leslie: That's a useful tool. I definitely need to manage the skills to improve communication.

Rachel: That's right. Memos are a convenient channel to communicate, but it is always necessary to determine if a meeting is more appropriate. For example, your staff need to make a very important financial decision. A memo can ask for that information from team members and request a response by a specific date.

Leslie: I see.

Rachel: Bear in mind, by meeting with everyone, however, you not only get to hear final decisions but the rationale behind them. In fact, new ideas may stem from face-to-face discussions. By writing a memo in this scenario, you may never come up with innovative ways of solving the problem.

Leslie: I think I need to figure out the purpose of writing a memo before actually doing so. That way I can decide if memos are the best communication channel.

Rachel: You're absolutely right.

Dialogue 2　Audience analysis

Some time later, Leslie asks Rachel for more information on memos.

Leslie: Rachel, I have noticed that sometimes the readers of my memo don't quite understand it. What should I do?

Rachel: Well, that's what we call "Audience Analysis". Normally, the readers of your memo are your co-workers and colleagues, but more often than before, you might also write memos to employees from other companies working on the project, or other departments within your company.

Leslie: But people outside our company may not be so familiar with the situation.

Rachel: Exactly. This is why knowing your audience is very essential when writing a memo. If your audience is generally familiar with you professionally and/or your role in the project, it is not necessary to provide a detailed background about the situation.

Leslie: What if they are new to the situation?

Rachel: If they are new, then you need to provide detailed background information so that they understand the situation and can provide constructive feedback if desired.

Leslie: What about the context? Is it necessary to provide it?

Rachel: Absolutely. Do not only write that a meeting will take place by listing the date and time. Inform why the meeting is occurring in the first place. Always include some way for them to get in touch with you and other members of the team working on the project.

Leslie: I agree. Last time I took it for granted that they had my phone number already, but it turned out I was wrong about that.

Rachel: In a word, always take the audience into consideration and take care of their needs. Only in that way can communication be conducted properly.

Dialogue 3   Memos' format

Rachel shares her knowledge on memos with Leslie, an intern.

Leslie: Rachel, what's the general format of a memo?

Rachel: Usually a memo has a "to", "from", "subject", and "date" entry. But a certain company might have a particular way of presenting a heading or may even use a specific type of letterhead or logo. We need to consider heading, tone, message and length when writing a memo.

Leslie: I see. What is a heading for?

Rachel: The heading is essential. It provides information about who will receive the memo, who is sending the memo, the date, and the memo's subject. This information may be bolded or highlighted in some way.

Leslie: Are there any suggestions to someone who's new?

Rachel: Well, if you are unsure, it may be a good idea to include your job title and your reader's. The memo will then be informative to someone new to the situation, or someone who received the memo after it was passed on from the original reader. Sometimes organizations specify how to fill out the headings.

Leslie: Sometimes I receive memos I don't quite understand. What do you think about that?

Rachel: I understand your situation. That's why it is important that the first sentence of the memo should answer that question with a purpose statement. The best purpose statements are concise and direct. When you're writing a memo, bear in mind your message should also provide a context for readers. In other words, always tell your readers why you are writing.

Leslie: It seems it's not easy to write a memo well. I think I'll have to practise more.

Rachel: I'm with you.

Ⅳ. Practice

Practice 1

Delegates from Bridge Stationery Co. are visiting the factory. Later the purchasing staff are expected to receive and have dinner with them. Write a memo to inform all the purchasing team of the arrangements.

Ss' example

Memo

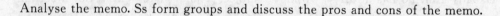

To: Purchasing staff
From: President Zhang's Office
Date: Sep. 3, 2009
Subject: Dinner arrangements

Dinner with the delegates from Bridge Stationery Co. is to be held at the College Hotel at 6 p. m. on Sep. 12, 2009. The President will deliver a welcome speech. Please take the opportunity to make more acquaintances. Your participation is appreciated.

Analyse the memo. Ss form groups and discuss the pros and cons of the memo.

Practice 2

A sports contest is held at Bridge Stationery Co. in November each year. Due to the inadequate facilities in the company, the event will be held in another location. Write a memo to inform all staff of the details.

Memo

To: All staff
From: President's Office
Date: Dec. 3, 2009
Subject: Change in sports contest

Due to the inadequate facilities in the company, the event will be held in another location in November. Please get ready for the event and wish you good results. We plan to build a sports stadium and hope all staff will make full use of it.

Analyse the memo. Ss form groups and discuss the pros and cons of the memo.

Practice 3

Due to the tough economic conditions around the world, some employees in each department will have to be laid off. Write a memo to the personnel director to discuss a way to minimize the tension and shock it may cause.

V. Course Project

Task 1

Some employees have arrived late for work. Write a memo to inform employees that neither being late nor leaving early is allowed in the company. Be sure to include all the points mentioned in the article.

Task 2

Complaints have been made on the tastes of the food in the canteen. Write a memo to cooks in the canteen and ask them to improve.

Task 3

Delegates from Officemate Trading are visiting our company. Write a memo to the sales team and ask them to show around the whole company.

Project 11
Meeting Minutes

I. Warming-Up

Task 1 Recognition.

Different equipment and tools are needed in order to record meeting minutes. Look at the following pictures carefully and decide what equipment or tool each picture shows.

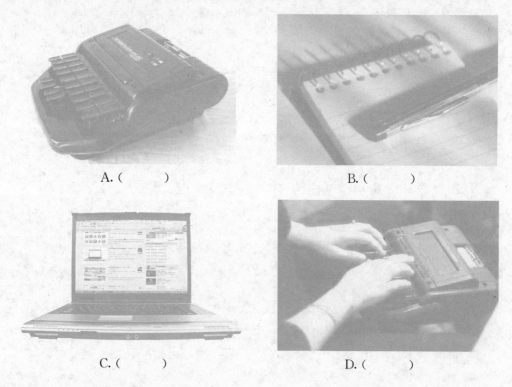

A. (　　) 　　　　　　 B. (　　)

C. (　　) 　　　　　　 D. (　　)

Task 2 Matching.

Match the English words and phrases with their Chinese counterparts.

1. Stenography　　　　　　a. 速记
2. Transcript　　　　　　　b. 速记员

3. Shorthand typist　　　　c. 转录，文字稿

4. Notebook　　　　　　　d. 会议记录

5. Meeting minutes　　　　e. 记事本

6. Business transactions　　f. 法庭诉讼

7. Court proceedings　　　g. 商业交易

8. Record　　　　　　　h. 记录

9. Participants　　　　　i. 董事会

10. Board meeting　　　　j. 参与人

11. Chief Executive Officer　k. 字迹清晰的

12. Skilled secretary　　　l. 首席执行官

13. Written records　　　　m. 经验十足的秘书

14. Tips for writing　　　　n. 写作指导

15. Legible　　　　　　　o. 书面记录

Ⅱ. Introduction to the Topic

Meeting Minutes

Minutes, also known as protocols, are the instant written record of a meeting or hearing. They often give an overview of the structure of the meeting, starting with a list of those present, a statement of the various issues before the participants, and each of their responses thereto. They are often created at the moment of the hearing by a typist or court recorder at the meeting, who may record the meeting in shorthand, and then prepare the minutes and issue them to the participants afterwards. Alternatively, the meeting may be audiorecorded or notes taken, and the minutes prepared later. However, it is often important for the minutes to be brief and concentrate on material issues rather than being a verbatim report, so the minute-taker should have sufficient understanding of the subject matter to achieve this. The minutes of certain entities, such as a corporate board of directors, must be kept and are important legal documents.

The following is a guide for making this task easier:

- Make sure that all of the essential elements are noted, such as type of meeting, name of the organization, date and time, name of the chair or facilitator, main topics and the time of adjournment. For formal and corporate meetings include approval of previous minutes, and all resolutions.
- Prepare an outline based on the agenda ahead of time, and leave plenty of white space for notes. By having the topics already written down, you can jump right on to a new topic without pause.
- Prepare a list of expected attendees and check off the names as people enter the room. Or,

you can pass around an attendance sheet for everyone to sign as the meeting starts.

- To be sure about who said what, make a map of the seating arrangement, and make sure to ask for introductions of unfamiliar people.
- Don't make the mistake of recording every single comment, but concentrate on getting the gist of the discussion and taking enough notes to summarize it later. Remember that minutes are the official record of what happened, not what was said, at a meeting.
- Use whatever device is comfortable for you, a notepad, a laptop computer, a tape recorder, a steno pad, shorthand. Many people routinely record important meetings as a backup to their notes.
- Be prepared! Study the issues to be discussed and ask a lot of questions ahead of time. If you have to fumble for understanding while you are making your notes, they won't make any sense to you later.
- Don't wait too long to type up the minutes, and be sure to have them approved by the chair or facilitator before distributing them to the attendees.
- Don't be intimidated, you may be called upon many times to write meeting minutes, and the ability to produce concise, coherent minutes is widely admired and valued.

Example of Minutes Format

Bridge Stationery Co. , Ltd.

BOARD MEETING MINUTES
October 14, 2008

The Kathy Collins convened the meeting at 7:18 p. m. Board members present at this meeting: Paul Whalen, Kathy Collins, and Keith DeWindt.

Minutes of the last Board meeting were approved by E-mail.

Secretary/Treasurer's Reports: Paul stated he E-mailed the financials prior to the meeting and said "we are solvent".

Paul reported that the delivery for last month was going well. Retailers are happy...

Staff living conditions:
Drainage for Staff Residential Bldg-Brad and Kathy did a check on the site. Paul discovered that a drainage near Bldg No. 1 is chronically flooded during a heavy rain. His solution is to install 2 small pumps or storm drains, i. e. PVC, level to the ground so as to be non-obtrusive...

The annual meeting will be held on Tuesday, January 20, 2009 at 7:30 p. m. Paul suggested it be held at the Bridge Conference Center. Paul motioned that the annual meeting be held at the same location. Keith seconded. All approved. Paul will reserve the meeting room and the charge will probably be around $100 for the evening.

Special Events: Cathy mentioned the factory is having difficulty with recruiting new staff due to the shortage of skilled workers. The remaining event planned for 2008 is the Holiday Gala. Group cookout

---

will possibly be held in March instead of November. The only other events they want to have is at Tomb-sweeping Festival. Paul motioned that the Holiday Gala be held on Friday Dec. 12. Keith seconded. All approved.

Paul motioned to adjourn at 8:40 p. m. Keith seconded. All approved.

Submitted by,

Paul

Bridge Stationery Co. , Ltd.

Exercise: True or False

1. _____ Minutes are on-the-site recordings of a meeting or a hearing.

2. _____ A typist or court recorder note down the meetings or hearings and distribute the minutes to the participants afterwards.

3. _____ It is advised that the recorder should write down every sentence said during a meeting or hearing.

4. _____ Usually a typist or recorder doesn't have to write down the topics for the meeting before it takes place.

5. _____ Nowadays recording equipment are also used to help record a meeting or hearing.

Ⅲ. Situational Dialogue

Dialogue 1　Meeting minutes

Rachel is recently assigned the task of writing down meeting minutes. She asks her colleague John for tips.

Rachel: Hi, John, I know that you have been writing meeting minutes for some time. I've just taken over. Could I ask some questions about meeting minutes?

John: Sure. Go ahead.

Rachel: What are the main elements within meeting minutes?

John: Well, participants present, the issues and reports discussed, and people's opinions and measures, if any, to be taken. Of course, information such as date, place etc should also be included.

Rachel: Right. And what should I prepare before the meeting?

John: First, remember to bring a pen and notebook to the meeting. Second, find out who is attending the meeting and third, be clear about the purpose of the meeting.

Rachel: Yeah, to have some idea of the meeting beforehand is surely necessary. What about in the meeting? Any advice?

John: Don't try to write down everything that is said, and focus only on the important (key) points in the meeting. Besides, note agreements and any special planning that is taking place. Basically, write down who is talking, what they are talking about, and when they said they were going to do something.

Rachel: I see. Oh, I almost forgot, the meeting is about to begin. Gotta go. Talk to you after the meeting.

John: Good luck.

Rachel: Thanks.

Dialogue 2   What went wrong

Rachel did the meeting minutes and met John.

John: Hay, Rachel, how did it go?

Rachel: Terrible. I did as you told me, but it seems I simply couldn't write down all the details. The speakers were talking real fast.

John: Oh, poor you. That's OK. After all, it's your first task.

Rachel: Of course it's easy for you to say so. But I was so nervous and embarrassed at the meeting. My hand was writing non-stop throughout the meeting.

John: I bet the speakers were making it hard for you. Well, when the participants are talking real fast, I just focus on only the important (key) points in the meeting. It's almost an impossible mission trying to take down each and every word being said.

Rachel: Actually, I had another problem. I didn't hear quite clearly what the members said. One director had a cold and his speech was interrupted by intermittent coughs. It was really hard for me to get his structure, you know, like where to stop a sentence.

John: My sympathies. I had similar experiences. If you are confused by anything, ask them right away even before the meeting is over. Once the meeting is done, start working on a draft because you don't want to have forgotten anything as we tend to do as time passes.

Rachel: Apparently I need to practise more often. One problem I find quite disturbing is my draft doesn't seem so logical. What would you do with that?

John: Divide your draft so that you are numbering and listing important points that were discussed and the way it was to be handled. All topics that are alike, group together and put under one heading. This should take a while before you can manage.

Rachel: Right. Thank you so much.

John: You are welcome.

Dialogue 3　On training

Rachel wrote meeting minutes for some time and found more confidence in herself.

John: Hay, Rachel, how are things going?

Rachel: Pretty good actually. You know, now I'm not so nervous when writing meeting minutes for the directors.

John: Glad to hear that. Practice makes perfect.

Rachel: It is certainly true with that saying. Now I sit as close as possible to the person who is conducting the meeting. In that way I can hear clearly what he/she says. They might have something important to put it and that needs to get added in the minutes, you know.

John: Good idea. That's very clever of you. Surely you're making lots of progress.

Rachel: Well, don't give me all the credit. Your tips are certainly helpful. I try my best to memorise all the useful tips: remember to write down what was dealt with well doing the meeting, not just the problems; itemize my draft so that it is formatted by: issues talked about, persons responsible, the dates that were agreed upon, and when the problems will be resolved.

John: Exactly. And finally, don't try to record everything that takes place within the meeting, it is an impossible task. Oh, one more thing, make sure you proofread your rough copy, afterwards mail it to the people who attended the meeting. If you miss that last step, you may find spelling mistakes within. That could be embarrassing as well.

Rachel: Right. I need to take that down before I forget.

John: Just remember, keeping track of minutes is a very significant task for a secretary. Think about it, if there were no minutes recorded then how will one be able to keep abreast of the topics discussed in regular meetings. But I'm confident that a diligent learner like you will surely manage all the necessary skills and stand out.

Rachel: Thank you. Let me buy you a drink after work.

John: It's long overdue.

Ⅳ. Practice

Practice 1

Following the format below, Rachel is expected to fill in the blanks for the Board Meeting on April 23, 2009.

Great Stationery Co. , Ltd.
MINUTES OF A MEETING OF THE BOARD OF DIRECTORS

Directors Present:

Directors Absent:

Counsel Present:

Call to Order

[Insert name of CEO or board chair]called the meeting to order at [Insert start time of meeting]and [Insert name of secretary]recorded the minutes. A quorum of directors was present, and the meeting, having been duly convened, was ready to proceed with business.

CEO Report

[Insert name of CEO]reviewed the agenda and welcomed everyone to the meeting. Next, [Insert name of CEO]discussed the current status of the company and its progress. A number of questions were asked and extensive discussion ensued.

Approval of Minutes

_____

Closed Session

The Board next discussed a number of strategic topics. Questions were asked and answered.

Adjournment

There being no further business to come before the meeting, the meeting was adjourned at [Insert time of adjournment].

Respectfully submitted,

Recording Secretary

Practice 2

The first part of this meeting minutes is missing. You are expected to complete this record.

Great Stationery Co. , Ltd.

_____

Call to Order

[Insert name of CEO or board chair]called the meeting to order at [Insert start time of meeting]and [Insert name of secretary]recorded the minutes. A quorum of directors was present, and the meeting, having been duly convened, was ready to proceed with business.

Sales & Business Development Update

[Insert name]next provided an update on the overall sales progress and sales pipeline of the Company. He also presented the status of business development discussions.

Approval of Minutes

[Insert name]presented to the Board the minutes of the [insert date of previous board meeting]meeting of the Board for approval, whereupon motion duly made, seconded and unanimously adopted, the minutes were approved as presented.

Closed Session

The Board next discussed a number of strategic topics. Questions were asked and answered.

Adjournment

There being no further business to come before the meeting, the meeting was adjourned at [Insert time of adjournment].

Respectfully submitted,

Recording Secretary

Practice 3

The shorthand typist is expected to complete the following minutes.

Officemate Stationery Co. ,Ltd.

Financial Review
[Insert name]provided a comprehensive update on the Company's financial plan and forecast. [Insert name]also reviewed the Company's principal financial operating metrics. Discussion ensued.
Financial Planning
The Board next discussed the timing and creation of the 2007 Operating Plan.
Approval of Option Grants
[Insert name]presented to the Board a list of proposed options to be granted to Company employees [and advisors], for approval, whereupon motion duly made, seconded and unanimously adopted, the option grants were approved as presented in Exhibit A.

V. Course Project

Task 1

Delegates from Officemate Trading Co. , Ltd. are meeting the senior management of Great Stationery Co. ,Ltd. Write meeting minutes for the event.

Task 2

Delegates from Bridge Stationery Co. , Ltd. are having a business meeting with the managers of Great Stationery Co. ,Ltd. to talk about areas of cooperation. Include details in the meeting minutes.

Task 3

An all-staff meeting is held at Great Stationery Co. , Ltd. CEO and staff representative delivered speeches in the event. Make meeting minutes for the event.

Project 12

Business Report

Task 1   Recognition.

There are different ways to present a business report clearly. Look at the following pictures carefully and decide what kind of charts each belong to.

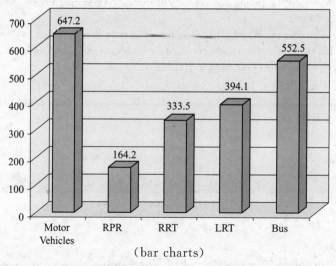

(bar charts)

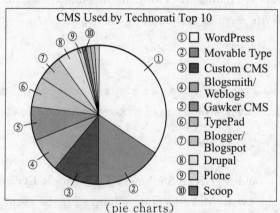

(pie charts)

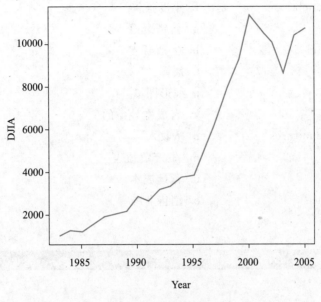

（graph）

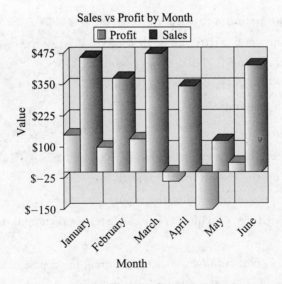

（sales bar charts）

Task 2　Matching.

Match the English words and phrases with their Chinese counterparts.

1. Bar chart
2. Graph
3. Pie chart

a. 饼图
b. 销售预测
c. 柱形图

4. Product range   d. 产品系列

5. Sales forecast   e. 发展趋势

6. Distribution channels   f. 年度报告

7. Annual report   g. 营销渠道

8. Development trend   h. 生产开支

9. Net income   i. 预算

10. Operating costs   j. 线形图

11. Budget   k. 有成本效益的

12. Production expenditures   l. 净收入

13. Cost-effective   m. 资产负债表

14. Balance sheet   n. 营运成本

15. Sales performance   o. 销售业绩

Ⅱ. Introduction to the Topic

Business Report

In business, the information provided in reports needs to be easy to find, and written in such a way that the client can understand it. This is one reason why reports are divided into sections clearly labelled with headings and sub-headings.

A report is divided into four areas:

- Terms of Reference—This section gives background information on the reason for the report. It usually includes the person requesting the report.

- Procedure—The procedure provides the exact steps taken and methods used for the report.

- Findings—The findings point out discoveries made during the course of the report investigation.

- Conclusions—The conclusions provide logical conclusions based on the findings.

- Recommendations—The recommendations state actions that the writer of the report feels need to be taken based on the findings and conclusions.

Useful phrases for writing reports:

Introduction

This report aims/sets out to...

The aim of this report is to...

Findings

It was found that…

Adding ideas

Furthermore/in addition…

Conclusion

It was concluded/decided/agreed that…

In conclusion,…

Recommendations

It is recommended/suggested that …

The following is one example observing such a format.

Report

Terms of Reference

Margaret Lin, Manager of Personnel of Officemate Stationery Co. , Ltd. has requested this report on employee benefits satisfaction. The report was to be submitted to her by 28 June.

Procedure

A representative selection of 15% of all employees were interviewed in the period between April 1st and April 15th concerning:

- Overall satisfaction with our current benefits package.
- Problems encountered when dealing with the personnel department.
- Suggestions for the improvement of communication policies.
- Problems encountered when dealing with our Social Security System(SSS).

Findings

- Employees were generally satisfied with the current benefits package.
- Some problems were encountered when requesting vacation due to what is perceived as long approval waiting periods.
- Older employees repeatedly had problems with SSS.
- Employees between the ages of 22 and 30 report few problems with SSS.
- Most employees complain about the lack of dental insurance in our benefits package.
- The most common suggestion for improvement was for the ability to enjoy benefits in cities other than the one you deposit your monthly sum with.

Conclusions

- Older employees, those over 50, are having serious problems with our SSS.
- Our benefits request system needs to be revised as most complaints concerning in-house processing.
- Improvements need to take place in personnel department response time.
- Information technology improvements should be considered as employees become more technologically savvy.

Recommendations

- Meet with SSS staff to discuss the serious nature of complaints for older employees.
- Give priority to vacation request response time as employees need faster approval in order to be able to plan their vacations.
- Take no special actions for the benefits package of younger employees.

■ **Note：**

Social security is an integral part in the efforts to promote social stability and economic development. The social security system is designed to provide material compensation or aid to help citizens overcome difficulties in their livelihood and unexpected disaster.

Exercise：True or False

1. _____Business reports should be easy to read and understand.
2. _____ A business report is usually divided into 4 parts.
3. _____ The opening part of a report is usually the findings.
4. _____ The last part, Recommendations, offers suggestions and advice.
5. _____ The example report discusses issues on employees' satisfaction on social security.

Ⅲ. Situational Dialogue

Dialogue 1　A business report

President Zhang called Rachel, his secretary, about a business report.

Zhang：This is President Zhang. Is Rachel in?

Rachel：This is Rachel speaking.

Zhang：Listen, the Board Meeting is due to begin and I need you to write a business report for me please.

Rachel：Sure. What's it about?

Zhang：Well, we've been through a tough year, I want you to prepare all the data on sales volume, net income and figures like that, you know.

Rachel：No problem. I'll get to it as soon as I've booked the airport for you.

Zhang：Great. Let's get started.

Dialogue 2　The board meeting

Both President Zhang and his secretary Rachel are at the meeting.

Zhang：　Ladies and gentlemen, I'm honored to present to you the sales graph and explain the whole picture a little bit. As you can see, we had a tough year. The main reason is of course the financial crisis. I want you to spend some time reading through all the graphs and charts before you raise questions.

(*After a while.*)

Margaret: President Zhang, would you clarify on the current operating expenses?

Zhang: Sure. As you can see, the biggest chunk of operating expenses come from the factory. We have several factories to run and that costs us a large amount of money. I think we are lucky that we don't experience so many strikes as our western counterparts do.

Lin: What's the sales like this year?

Zhang: Well, for this year, due to the massive economic stimulus package, we're seeing better signs. Our sales are climbing steadily compared with last year. We hope to tap into the current recovery and turn our sales round. But that would require all your efforts and also the hard work of our sales team.

Lin: President Zhang, what role should the internet play this year? Are we gonna use internet more?

Zhang: Definitely. We've noticed that online commerce is playing a bigger role in China. And we've seen online discussions about our products. We aim to increase online sales and improve our image at the same time.

Dialogue 3   After the board meeting

Rachel and Robert discuss on the techniques of writing a business report.

Rachel: Robert, can I ask you some questions on business report writing? I know you are quite knowledgeable and proficient in writing reports.

Robert: Sure. Go ahead.

Rachel: What are the main types of business reports?

Robert: They include general business report, business plan and proposal, financial plan, financial analysis, and others.

Rachel: Are there any differences among these reports?

Robert: Well, the technical content and terminology will vary from report to report, depending on the subject and industry context, but the actual "report writing process" will be essentially the same.

Rachel: I see. What should I do first?

Robert: First, decide on the outcome and expectations for a report. When determining this, always think specifically in terms of the final deliverable (usually the final report). What issues must it address? What direction/guidance is it expected to give? What exactly will it contain? What bottom line are they looking for?

Rachel: What next? Shall I do some research?

Robert: How smart of you. You're supposed to conduct initial pre-report research. This stage may be as simple as collecting and reading a few background documents, or it could involve developing questionnaires and conducting detailed interviews with the appropriate people. Then you'll start to prepare the draft report.

Rachel: Right, thank you for your advice.

Ⅳ. Practice

Practice 1

You have recently visited Ningbo Beifa Group, a potential supplier of writing instruments as well as stationery in China. Look at the memo below and the handwritten notes. Then write a report recommending whether your company should deal with the supplier or not. Make sure your report cover all the handwritten notes.

To: Rachel

Fm: Jack

Date: Feb. 24, 2009

Re: Your visit to Beifa Group

Rachel,

Here's the information about Beifa. Beifa Group was established on January 8th, 1994, started as a pen and stationery trade company. In 2000, Beifa Group invested USD 15 million and built the world's largest plant in writing instrument industry.

Can you find out the following and write a report recommending what we should do?

The factory

- production facilities? ——

- production capacity? ——

> Modern equipment
> high capacity

Products

- product range? ——

> Wide range

Production times

- delivery times? ——

> On time

Hope you can finish the report in time. Good luck.

Practice 2

You have recently visited Ningbo Beifa Group and you have written your own report. Now compare yours with this one and write down the differences.

Report on suitability of Ningbo Beifa Group

Introduction

This report aims to assess whether Ningbo Beifa Group would be a suitable supplier of stationery for us.

Findings

A recent visit to the company and its factory showed that its facilities are modern, which promises high capacity. Furthermore, Beifa produces a wide range of stationery goods including pens, papers and scissors.

In addition, its updated machinery and efficient staff guarantees on-time delivery of goods.

Conclusion

Beifa would be suitable for large orders requiring immediate delivery.

Practice 3

You have visited Officemate Stationery Co. , Ltd. and you're expected to write a report on whether it is suitable to be your long-term business partner. You should follow the pattern below.

Contents

The Contents of the report should be consistently laid out throughout the report and you should include both page numbers and title numbers.

Introduction

The introduction should say why the report is being written. Reports are nearly always written to solve a business problem. Reports maybe commissioned because there is a crisis or they maybe routine. Nearly all reports in some way answer the age-old business problem, how can we increase profits?

Findings

Sometimes reports don't say Findings, but it is normally assumed that the main part of your report will be the information you have found.

This information is not always read by executives, but that doesn't mean it isn't important, because without thorough research and analysis the author will not be able to come to effective conclusions and create recommendations. Also if anything in the executive summary surprises the executive, then they will turn directly to the relevant part of the recommendations.

Conclusions

The conclusions should summarize the Findings section, do not include diagrams or graphs in this area. This area should be short, clearly follow the order of the findings and lead naturally into the recommendations.

Recommendations

All reports should include recommendations or at least suggestions. It is important to make sure that there is at least an indicator of what the Return on Investment would be. It is always best if this can be directly linked, but may not always be possible.

Make sure that your recommendations clearly follow what is said in the conclusions.

Ⅴ. Course Project

Task 1

Great Stationery Co., Ltd. requires a bus firm that it could use on a regular basis to pick up both staff and clients. After selecting an advertisement from the local newspaper with the handwritten notes, write a report on the firm.

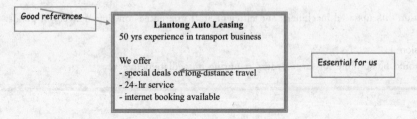

Task 2

Recently your company has been carrying out an environmental campaign intended to improve the river conditions. Write a report on the environment-friendly measures your company has taken so far.

Task 3

Officemate Stationery Co., Ltd. requires a bus firm that it could use to pick up clients. Write a report on the advantages and disadvantages of this company.

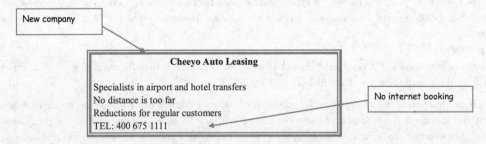

Project 13

Meeting Guests at the Airport

Ⅰ. Warming-Up

Task 1　Picture recognition.

Can you name the function areas in the picture?

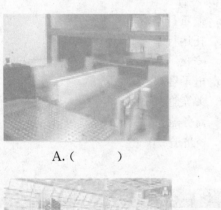

A. (　　　)

B. (　　　)

C. (　　　)

D. (　　　)

E. (　　　)

F. (　　　)

Task 2   Matching.

Match the English words and phrases with their Chinese counterparts.

1. visa
2. carry-on articles/cabin baggage
3. baggage trolley/cart
4. the conveyor belt
5. baggage claim
6. passport
7. excess baggage charge
8. health card
9. first class
10. boarding pass
11. electronic ticket
12. baggage tag
13. departure lounge/waiting hall
14. domestic flight
15. business class
16. direct flight
17. estimated time of arrival
18. economy class
19. security check
20. check-in baggage

a. 登机牌
b. 国内航班
c. 直达航班
d. 手提行李
e. 行李搬运车
f. 行李牌
g. 行李认领处
h. 候机厅
i. 预计到达时间
j. 健康证
k. 传输带
l. 护照
m. 签证
n. 逾重行李费
o. 托运行李
p. 安检
q. 电子客票
r. 头等舱
s. 商务舱
t. 经济舱

Ⅱ. Introduction to the Topic

Meeting Guests at the Airport

The checklist to prepare before meeting guests at the airport：

a. Guests lists, with person in charge noted.

b. Information about visitors' background, including their customs and taboos, likes and dislikes.

c. Knowledge of visitors' objectives and their desired itinerary.

d. Confirmation with the places to be visited.

e. Booking information：the hotel, coach, meals, the attractions, transportation for next stop.

f. Coupons to the restaurants and attractions, tickets.

g. Checks or vouchers for payment.

h. Name badge (to identify yourself).

i. Sign board, with guests' name and flight details clearly printed or written.

Procedures to remember when meeting guests at the airport:

–Come to the airport at least 30 minutes in advance; check the arrival terminal to confirm the actual arrival time and arrival gate.

–Ensure the limousine picking up the guests arrives at the airport 15 minutes prior to the flight arrival.

– Know the location of the baggage claim area.

–Hold the signboard in front of you at eye visible level, and stand in front of the arrival gate to wait for the guest.

–Receive the guests and offer a friendly greeting, inquire about their trip, and give brief but clear instructions as to the immediate procedures.

–Help guests when they collect their luggage, and remind them to check if there is any damage. And then transfer the luggage to the vehicle.

– Escort the visitors to the limousine.

Relevant etiquette when receiving guests:

– Make sure you are clean and tidy.

– On a formal occasion, it is best to dress in black and blue.

–Don't be humble or pushy, but show respect for them and their customs.

– Be punctual and keep your promise.

– When shaking hands, you can use a little strength, but not too tightly.

– You should always use "please, thanks" in your talks.

– Always maintain a smile.

– After obtaining guest name, you must greet guest by name.

– Get ready to help your guests before they are in trouble.

–Let the guest walk on the right. It's polite for you to open the door and let them go through the door first.

– Do not ask about age, salary and other private matters.

– Do not smoke unless you are permitted.

Exercise: True or False

1. _____ You should know visitors' objectives before you meet them.
2. _____ When meeting guests at the airport, you should reach the airport on time.
3. _____ Black and blue are always good choices for colors of suits on formal occasions.
4. _____ You should shake hands with a lot of strength.
5. _____ When going through the door, the host should go first.

Ⅲ. Situational Dialogue

Dialogue 1　Picking up guests from the airport

A: Excuse me, are you Mr. Paul King, the CEO of Officemate Trading Co. , Ltd. ?

B: Yes. And you are...

A: I've been expecting you. I'm Wang Ling, secretary to Mr. Li Jian, President of Deli Group. Nice to meet you. And welcome to Ningbo, China.

B: Nice to meet you, too. Thank you for coming to meet us.

A: It's my pleasure. How was your trip?

B: We were held up for a few hours at Hong Kong Airport because of a small accident. But on the whole we had a smooth flight.

A: I'm glad you had a nice trip.

B: By the way, where do we pick up the luggage?

A: This way, please.

(*They go to the luggage claim area and get the luggage.*)

A: Have you got all of your luggage?

B: Yeah.

A: May I help you with your suitcase?

B: Oh, thank you, but I can manage it myself.

A: Good, now let's go to the car. Please follow me.

A: Would you please put them in the trunk?

B: Oh, sure. Is that OK?

A: OK.

(*Now they are in the car.*)

A: Please fasten your seat belt. We will soon be on the expressway.

B: Can I talk with Mr. Li Jian, President of Sunshine Group right away?

B: Mr. Li Jian is really looking forward to talking with you. But for now, I think you must be tired after this long flight, so we'd better go straight to the hotel, where you can get settled.

Dialogue 2　At the customs

Customs Officer: Excuse me, can I see your passport?

Foreigner: Of course, here it is, sir.

Customs Officer: And your visa, please.

(*The customs officer checks the papers carefully, and return them to him.*)

Customs Officer: Very good, your papers are all in order. Where are you going to stay?

Foreigner: I'm going to stay in Ninbo hotel.

Customs Officer: How long are you staying in Ningbo?

Foreigner: For about weeks.

Customs Officer: Have you got anything to declare?

Foreigner: I've got some money, one camera, and some presents for my family.

Customs Officer: What have you got in your cases?

Foreigner: My clothes. Shall I open the case?

Customs Officer: No, that's all right. Hope you will enjoy your stay in China.

Note:

Directly after claiming the luggage, all passages must go through immigration, where travelers must show their passports and visas. Customs regulates what travelers bring in and out of the country.

Dialogue 3   At the information desk

A: Excuse me?

B: Yes? Is there anything I can do for you?

A: Where is the luggage claim area?

B: Go straight along the hallway. At the end of the hallway, turn left.

A: Go down the hall way, and then turn left. Is that right?

B: That's right. And you will find the luggage claim area on the right.

A: I see. One more question, how will I know where to find my luggage?

B: On which flight did you just arrive?

A: United Airline flight 445 from Britain.

B: You will find you luggage on carousel number three.

A: Thanks a lot.

B: My pleasure.

Ⅳ. Practice

Make dialogues according to the following situations.

Practice 1

Student A: You are Li Tong, secretary in ABC Company. You boss, Mr. Zhang Ming, asks you to meet Mr. Bill Smith, the sales representative of the supplier, Eco-Office Trading Co. in France, at the airport.

Student B: You are Mr. Bill Smith.

Practice 2

Student A: You are David Brown, Purchasing Manager of Rainbow Company. You are paying a business trip to Shanghai. You have just claimed your luggage and you are stopped by a customs officer.

Student B: You are the customs officer. You stop David Brown, ask to see his passport and visa, ask him whether he has anything to declare, and let him open the suitcase to have a check.

Practice 3

Student A: You are a foreign traveler. You have just arrived at Ningbo Airport. You don't know the location of the luggage claim area and the bus terminal. So you go to the information desk to ask the way.

Student B: You are clerk at the information desk. You answer the traveler's questions carefully and patiently.

V. Course Project

Paul King, CEO of Officemate Trading Co., Ltd. in Great Britain, is paying a business visit to Great Stationery Co., Ltd. He will arrive in Ningbo tomorrow afternoon.

Mr. Zhang, president of Great Stationery Co., Ltd., asks Rachel to meet Paul King at the airport.

Task 1

Rachel is making a list of things she should do before going to the airport.

```
                            Checklish
        Confirmation of hotel reservation
        _____
        _____
        _____
```

Task 2

Rachel is discussing the things she should pay attention to when meeting guests at the airport with Mr. Han Lin, the office dean.

Task 3

Rachel meets Paul King at the airport. She greets him friendly, inquires about his trip, and gives brief but clear explanation to the immediate arrangement. Then she helps him claim the luggage and sends him to the hotel.

Project 14
Company Presentation

Task 1   Picture recognition.

Do you know what companies these logos belong to? What product /service do these compa-nies provide? Can you briefly introduce these companies?

A. (   )   B. (   )   C. (   )

D. (   )   E. (   )   F. (   )

G. (   )   H. (   )

Task 2　Matching.

Match the English words and phrases with their Chinese counterparts.

1. multinational corporation		a. 企业形象	
2. transformation		b. 创业精神	
3. registered capital		c. 团队精神	
4. fair competition		d. 跨国公司	
5. corporate/enterprise image		e. 转型	
6. head-hunter		f. 注册资本	
7. infrastructure		g. 公平竞争	
8. enterprising spirit/pioneering spirit		h. 猎头公司	
9. international competitiveness		i. 人力资本	
10. joint venture		j. 资金密集型产业	
11. listed companies		k. 基础设施	
12. market share		l. 国际竞争力	
13. team spirit		m. 共同努力	
14. human capital		n. 合资企业	
15. strategic planning		o. 上市公司	
16. capital-intensive industries		p. 市场占有率、市场份额	
17. strong demand		q. 战略部署，战略计划	
18. joint effort		r. 需求强劲	
19. sunset industry		s. 批量生产	
20. mass production		t. 夕阳产业	

II. Introduction to the Topic

Company Presentation

The **corporate presentation**，also called company presentation，is one of the important ways that your company values and brand are communicated. A number of presenters may all need to present the same，or similar，slides. The same corporate presentation might need to be delivered in different settings，to different audiences，and at different levels. Many companies are let down by their corporate presentation. But whether you have a vast budget or no budget—there are some straightforward things that you can do to improve the effectiveness of your credentials presentation.

Here are ten tips for those developing corporate presentations，and those who have to deliver them.

1. **Set objectives.** Why are you delivering a corporate presentation? What do the audience think now，and what do you want them to think? What are the audience doing now，and

what do you want them to be doing? If you know the individuals—answer these questions for each key decision maker.

2. See things from the audience's point of view. Before you start putting together your slides, start thinking about what they want to hear and not what you want to tell them. Do they really care about the details of your company structure and your developing strategy? We've had clients who have insisted on showing a series of pictures of new office building and staff gym. Ask, does the audience care about this? What's in it for them?

3. If you can E-mail your corporate presentation to somebody who wasn't there to see you deliver it, and they can understand it—then you, as a presenter, aren't necessary. Unnecessary presenters struggle when delivering corporate presentations face-to-face (the audience can just read the slides instead).

4. Make your corporate presentation's key messages memorable. Most presentations make 100s of points, and this leads to most people forgetting most of your messages. What's worse, when you have a few people in the audience, they all remember different points. A logical structure is essential, and repetition is key.

5. **Another aspect of effective corporate presentation to be aware of is the phrase "show, don't tell".** People dislike being told, but enjoy being shown. This applies to a huge range of media and forms of communication. Even in writing, good novels tend to show the reader what is happening through action, interaction and dialog, and the best and most popular radio plays allow listeners to hear what is happening rather than simply narrate the action to them.

6. **No bullet points.** Most corporate presentations are packed with bullet points. The problem is that bullet points are a very inefficient way of telling a story. In a presentation 55% of the way that we take in information is visual compared with only 7% for text (bullet points). If you use images to tell your story then you will have an immediate competitive advantage. And if you are wondering about the other 38%, this is for vocal delivery. Use visual PowerPoint slides—charts, diagrams, animation, and photos to appear dynamic and up-to-date, and to get your point across.

7. **Tell stories, and use case studies.** Ideally, supply a few so that those delivering your presentation can use one relevant to each audience. Stories are memorable, and bring your messages to life. Stories recounting previous customer successes help to present credentials in an interesting way, and reassure prospects that you can do what you say you can.

8. Don't just list your products. Instead, **structure your presentation around the problems that your company can solve**, and the benefits that your company can deliver. Then, just talk about your products as you explain the different ways your company can deliver value. This might mean that one product gets mentioned in a few different places, but wouldn't you rather your prospect got interested in *all* the products that help solve a problem they are facing?

9. **Less is more.** You have lots to tell—you are brimming with enthusiasm—you want to pack all your information into a very short period of time. The problem is that too much

information can be a real turn off. Simplify your message and your audience will be able to understand it.

10. Avoid one-size-fits-all if it doesn't. Your company might not change much, but your prospects are all different. So, **build some flexibility into your corporate presentation.** There's a balance to find between presenting a clear and consistent message to the market, with tailoring your corporate presentation to different audiences. Try to make every prospect feel that you can solve *their* problems, and can offer what *they* need. Consider an interactive presentation if you want to have flexibility to quickly attract client interests.

Tips for the presenter

Dress for success. You wouldn't present wearing a shell suit—so make sure that you are dressed correctly. Generally speaking, it is better to dress on the smart side. You could also read our article about what to wear.

"Life is a stage and we are just players on it."

When we go up to present, we put ourselves on display. The audience will be looking at us—often in intense detail. Ensure that you have covered off the finer points—hair brushed, shoes cleaned, clothes ironed, nails cleaned and clipped.

Exercise: True or False

1. _____ You should study your clients before you prepare to present.

2. _____ To achieve better effect, you'd better do the corporate presentation face to face.

3. _____ During the presentation, you should tell your audience as much information about your company as possible.

4. _____ You can make some changes to the corporate presentation when presenting to different customers.

5. _____ You'd better wear a formal suit to show respect to the audience when you present.

Samples of company presentation

Sample 1

Post Danmark A/S can trace its history as far back as 1624 when King Christian Ⅳ signed a decree concerning the establishment of a network of postmen in Denmark. Ever since then, we have provided reliable, fast and inexpensive transport of mail in Denmark and abroad.

Post Danmark A/S today, about 67 per cent of Post Danmark's annual revenue of approximately DKK 11. 7 billion is generated by business areas which are in open and free competition with other undertakings.

Post Danmark competes with Danish and foreign postal service providers on management, economy as well as product mix. The company's focus is on the needs of its customers. Post

Danmark's mission is to provide basic postal services to all customers in Denmark—senders and recipients alike. Post Danmark's aim is to be the best postal service provider in Europe, measured in terms of service level, quality and price combined.

We are fast and provide high quality. Every day, Post Danmark's employees collect and sort a total of approximately 11 million items of mail for delivery among 5. 2 million customers distributed on 2. 6 million households. In several measurements, Post Danmark has proved to be fastest and to provide the best letter quality among European postal service providers. Approximately 95 per cent of all domestic letters handed in on time for delivery on the following business day are delivered as promised. Impartial quality checks are carried out continuously to monitor that our distribution areas and mail centers always live up to our high quality standards. Post Danmark will continue to be reckoned among the best postal, logistics and transport companies.

Post Danmark is an important business partner for commerce and industry. Light goods, business parcels and facility services are some of the important services that a large number of Danish under-takings use every day. Our customers cover the entire spectrum of Danish undertakings, from the largest well-established conglomerates to small newly established entrepreneurs.

We are approximately 21,000 employees. Post Danmark is one of Denmark's largest enterprises with approximately 21, 000 employees working in eight clearly defined business units. Our customers mainly meet Post Danmark via the country's approximately 900 post offices and post shops as well as via our postmen. The overall mechanical sorting of letters and parcels is carried out by a number of sorting centers around the country.

We are preparing for new challenges. Post Danmark owns or is the co-owner of a number of enterprises, including Budstikken Transport A/S (100 per cent), Post Danmark Leasing A/S (100 per cent), DATA SCANNING A/S (100 per cent), Pan Nordic Logistics AB (50 per cent) and e-Boks (33. 3 per cent). Since 1 January 2006, Post Danmark is jointly with CVC Capital Partners the co-owner of the Belgian postal service provider, De Post—La Poste, having purchased 50 per cent less one share of the company's capital. With effect from 1 January 2007, Post Danmark has purchased 51 per cent of the shares in Transport Group A/S.

In these years, Post Danmark is facing great new challenges. Customers are making greater demands on the postal service provided by Post Danmark. Competition has sharpened in the distribution, transport and logistics sectors. Post Danmark's monopoly is only for letters weighing up to and including 50 grams and is expected to be further reduced. The number of letters is falling. Post Danmark has taken these years' trends into account in its strategy, which describes the company's mission, vision and values.

Post Danmark's management development. Since 1998, Post Danmark has worked systematically to develop management forms and staff commitment in the company based on the

Excellence Model. Intensive efforts are being made to develop quality according to the EFQM standard (European Foundation for Quality Management). As a result of these efforts, Post Danmark received the Danish Quality Award in the spring of 2004. In 2006, Post Danmark was among the finalists in the competition for the EFQM Excellence Award.

Sample 2

we are...

... an international IT services company with core competences in the field of IT **infrastructure and outsourcing** for SMEs. Our main focus is strategically useful and proven solutions implemented with skill and in line with the requirements of the customer. We possess many years of expertise in the sphere of IT infrastructures and applications, we have the most up-to-date computer centres and we offer customised service management and IT outsourcing.

Our company motto—**a byte better**, characterises our daily thinking and practice and motivates us to perform better than average.

Our locations

WÜRTH|*ITensis*
...*a byte better*

Würth ITensis AG
Aspermontstrasse 1
CH-7000 Chur
Tel.+41 (0)81 558 30 00
Fax +41 (0)81 558 35 70

Würth ITensis AG
Sees mosse 39
CH-8700 küsnocht
TEl.+41(0)44 913 93 00
Fax +41 (0)44 913 93 01

Würth ITensis AG
Tanzbühlstrasse9
CH-7270 Daros
TEl. +41 (0)81 413 01 20
Fax +41 (0)81 558 35 70

Würth Group of North America
93 Grand streer
PO Box 357
US-Romsey ,NJ 07 446
Tel. +1 201 818 88 77
Fax +1 201 818 78 35

 Member of
the WurthGroup

W ü rth ITensis worldwide

WÜRTH|*ITensis*
...*a byte better*

- Registered office   Chur, Switzerland
- Core business   Services in the field of IT infrastructure and outsourcing
- Founded   1999
- Employees   8.5
- Locations   4 [Switzerland: Chur, Küsnacht, Davos and USA: Ramsey]
- Group   100% Würth subsidiary company
- Success factors   Practical relevance, security of investment, experience and quality

 Member of
the WurthGroup

The Würth Group worldwide

WÜRTH *ITensis*
...a byte better

- Registered office   Künzelsau, Germany
- Core business   Selling fixing and installation materials
- Founded   1946
- Employees   More than 63,000
- Locations   Over 425 companies in 84 countries
- 2006 turnover   EUR 8.8 billion
- Products   Over 100,000 products for industry and trade
- Culture   Major commitment in the field of art and culture

Member of
the Würth Group

The Würth Group Switzerland

WÜRTH *ITensis*
...a byte better

- Würth AG   Fixing and assembly technology
- Würth Finance International B.V   Group service provider for finances
- Würth Financial Services AG   Financial services
- Würth Industrie Service GmbH & Co.KG   Industrial supply
- Würth International AG   Central purchasing
- Würth ITensis AG   IT service provider
- Würth Leasing AG   Capital goods leasing
- Würth Logistics AG   Logistics service provider
- Würth Modyf AG   Work clothing
- Würth Promotional Concepts AG   Advertising media

Member of
the Würth Group

Our core competences

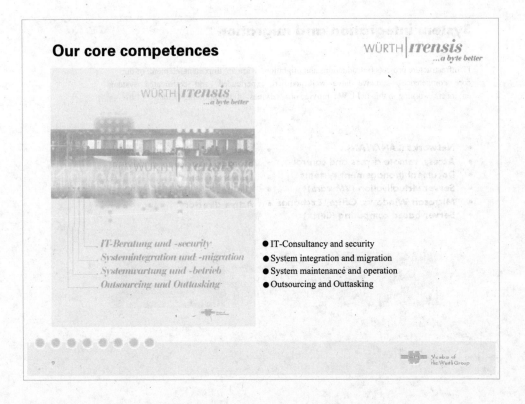

- IT-Consultancy and security
- System integration and migration
- System maintenance and operation
- Outsourcing and Outtasking

IT consultancy and security

"We only sell what we operate ourselves". This motto is based on the fact that all our services, products and solutions ane tested to their best in our own research centres. As a consultancy service, we make this expertise in technologies, service and IT security available to our customers. We are happy to advise you on:

- **System analysis and design**
- **System audits and reports**
- **Security audits**
- **Business continuity management**

System integration and migration

WÜRTH **ITensis**
...a byte better

IT infrastructure projects [introductions and migrations] are an important element of our core competence , and we have well-qualified, experienced and certificated system engineers working in this field. We provide our services in the following fields:

- **Networks (LAN/WAN)**
- **Access, remote access and control**
- **Document management systems**
- **Server virtualisation (VMware)**
- **Microsoft Windows, Office, Exchange**
- **Server-based computing (Citrix)**

- **Security (firewall, anti-virus)**
- **Storage / backup / archiving**
- **Server systems**
- **Clients (PCs, Thinclients, PDAs)**
- **Active directory**

Member of
the Würth Group

System maintenance and operation

WÜRTH **ITensis**
...a byte better

Numerous Swiss SMEs and the 370 companies of the Würth Group put their trust in our specialists. We can take over the support of individual areas or the whole IT infrastructure including applications that are critical to the company. We can provide services direct on-site or in our high-security computer centres. We offer you the following services:

- **Service Desk**
- **System management and monitoring**
- **System support (remote and on-site)**
- **Service Level Agreements (SLAs) and reporting**

Member of
the Würth Group

Outsourcing and out-tasking

With Würth ITensis outsourcing you can use your business applications in a reliable and secure environment [high-security computer centres] and this removes the need for in-house IT, leaving you completely free to concentrate on your core business. You receive guaranteed availability, IT security and transparency of costs for your IT. We offer the following outsourcing models:

- **IT out-tasking**
- **Transitional IT outsourcing**
- **Applications service providing (ASP)**
- **System housing**

- **IT-Outsourcing**
- **Complete IT-Outsourcing**
- **System Hosting**

13

Computer centres

A company outsourcing its systems for operation externally can expect a professional infrastructure, maximum security and optimum general conditions. Our computer centres are designed according to the highest security criteria and possess international quality certificates. Our computer centres guarantee the best protection from:

- **Water ingress**
- **Temperature and dust**
- **Unauthorised entry**
- **Power failures**

- **Fire**
- **Collapse**
- **Vandalism and explosion**

14

Logistics consulting

WÜRTH **ITensis**
...a byte better

The restructuring of the economy, intensifying competition and market dynamics require continuous logistical and process innovations for the company to remain in business. Moreover, increasing customer-orientation demands considerably greater flexibility in logistics. You can benefit from our many years of experience by using our logistic and IT expertise in the following areas:

- **Logistics auditing**
- **Planning of logistics systems**
- **Implementation and execution**
- **Project management**

15

Member of
the WurthGroup

Hardware and software business

WÜRTH **ITensis**
...a byte better

We have continuously optimised the IT components business over the last few years and we now co-operate with a selection of the best-in-class suppliers of technology, allowing us to offer a full service for procurement, replacement and exchange of IT infrastructures and software.

The **Würth ITensis online ordering shopping portal** is available should you wish to buy over the Internet speedily, cost-effectively and reliably.

16

Member of
the WurthGroup

System solutions

Our system solutions are to be understood as "best practice solutions", which we have further developed into standard solutions based on our experience in various customer projects. Our customers thus benefit from standardised and practically proven systems. We offer the following system solutions:

- **Würth ITensis VPN connect**   (Secure data connection)
- **Würth ITensis back-up housing**   (Back-up outsourcing)
- **Würth ITensis Neteye system monitoring**   (System monitoring)
- **Würth ITensis managed firewall**   (Full service for firewall system)
- **EASY ENTERPRISEx**   (Document management)
- **EASY xBase**   (E-mail archiving)
- **EASY xSTORE file archiving**   (File archiving)
- **Push mail**   (Mobile computing)
- **User portal**   (Remote access and control)

17   Member of the WürthGroup

Our partners

EMC²	Technology partner	www.emc.com
IBM	Technology partner	www.ibm.com
hp invent	Technology partner	www.hp.com
AASTRA	Technology partner	www.aastra.ch
cablecom	Technology partner	www.cablecom.ch
Check Point	Technology partner	www.checkpoint.com
CISCO	Technology partner	www.cisco.com
CITRIX	Technology partner	www.citrix.de

18   Member of the WürthGroup

III. Situational Dialogue

Dialogue 1

Susan, secretary to the General Manager of a stationery factory, meets Paul, sales manager from one of the client companies, at the gate of the factory.

Susan: Nice to see you again, Paul. Welcome to our factory.

Paul: Nice to see you, Susan. Glad to visit your factory. Could you give a general picture of your factory?

Susan: Our factory was founded in 1978 and now has 7 workshops and 5 administrative departments with 3,842 employees. The products enjoy high reputation and sell well both at home and abroad.

Paul: What's your annual production?

Susan: Approximately 70,000.

Paul: What's your market share?

Susan: I guess it's about 28%. We're the third largest stationery manufacturer in China.

Paul: Have the workshops been kept busy?

Susan: Yes. Very busy. All the workshops take three shifts a day.

Paul： Can we look around the workshops now?

Susan： Sure. Follow me, please.

Dialogue 2

Now Susan and Paul are viewing the manufacturing process in the workshop.

Susan： Put on the gloves, please.

Paul： Why?

Susan： For the sake of security. To protect your hand. It's one of the security regulations.

Paul： Thanks. Are these equipment imported?

Susan：Some are home made and some are imported. They are introduced just to improve the quality of products and reduce labor intensity for workers.

Paul： Is the production line fully automated?

Susan： Well, not fully.

Paul： I see. Does your factory carry out the entire process of manufacturing?

Susan： Almost. A few necessary items are made else where. Then they are checked for quality at our factory.

Paul： What kind of quality control do you have?

Susan： It's extremely strict. Quality is one of our primary considerations.

Paul： That's the way it should be. By the way, do you have any samples of products?

Susan： Yes. Go to the sample room, please.

Dialogue 3

Now Susan and Paul are looking at the products in the sample room.

Paul： What stationery do you produce?

Susan： Our products fall into five categories. They are staplers, calculators, pens, pencil sharpeners, paper shredders and paper products.

Paul： Paper products? Can you introduce in details?

Susan： Please come over here. Look, we produce a variety of paper products, such as printing paper, note books, memo pads and paper shopping bags. All of them come in different sizes.

Paul： Ah, I see. And what about pens?

Susan： Go over there. We mainly produce ballpoint pens, highlight pens and gel pens. You can have a lot of colors to choose from.

Paul： Oh, the pencil sharpeners are so amazing. Can you produce with customers' samples?

Susan： Of course. Whatever shape and color your samples are, we can produce without any difference.

Paul： That's great. Do you process with customers' material?

Susan: We seldom do it. But if you stick to it, we may discuss.

Paul: Thank you very much for your kind introduction. May I have a talk with your General Manager?

Susan: Yeah, he's already in the office expecting you.

IV. Practice

Before the class, you should study a well-known company in China, and jot down all the important information about it.

In the class, make dialogues according to the following situations, with the information you get beforehand.

Practice 1

Student A: You are Li Fang, secretary of the company. You are introducing the overall situation of your company to Bill Smith who is a client.

Student B: You are Bill Smith, the client. And you are interested in the history, the present situation and the future development of the company.

Practice 2

Student A: You are Li Fang, secretary of the company. You are showing Mr. Bill Smith, the client, around the company.

Student B: You are Mr. Bill Smith, the client. When you are shown around the company, you raise some questions.

Practice 3

Student A: You are Li Fang, secretary of the company. You are showing Mr. Bill Smith, the client, the sample room of the company.

Student B: You are Mr. Bill Smith, the client. You are interested in the products and talk about the possible cooperation.

V. Course Project

Paul King, CEO of Officemate Trading Co., Ltd. in Great Britain, is paying a business visit to Great Stationery Co., Ltd.

Mr. Zhang, president of Great Stationery Co., Ltd., asks Rachel to receive Paul King and introduce the company.

Task 1

Rachel is discussing the things to note when presenting the company with Mr. Han Lin, the office dean.

Task 2

Rachel is introducing the general situation of Great Stationery Co., Ltd. to Paul King, with the use of PPT.

Task 3

Rachel is comparing the situation of Great Stationery and their rival company Roy Maximum, with the information below.

Great Stationery	Roy Maximum
taking more staff	is declaring redundancies
enjoy steady growth	has a falling turnover
make profit	is making heavy losses
is in credit and has no liquidity problems	has an overdraft and cash-flow problems
has an increased market share	has a reduced market share
is launching new products	has a limited product range
enjoys high productivity	is inefficient in production
has a capital investment program	can't afford new investment
has good workforce morale	suffers from industrial unrest
is highly competitive	is no longer competitive
seems a sound and reliable investment	seems a high-risk investment
has a secure future	may soon collapse / go bankrupt

Source: http://www. m62. net/presentation-theory/presentation-best-practice/corporate-presentation-tips/
http://www. postdanmark. dk/cms/en-us/aboutus/companypresentation/Company_presentation. htm
www. cpugcon. com/.../CPUG_2009_Company_Presentation_WuerthITensis. pdf-, 2010-12-30

Product Presentation

Task 1   Picture recognition.

Can you name the stationery in the following pictures? What else do you know about them?

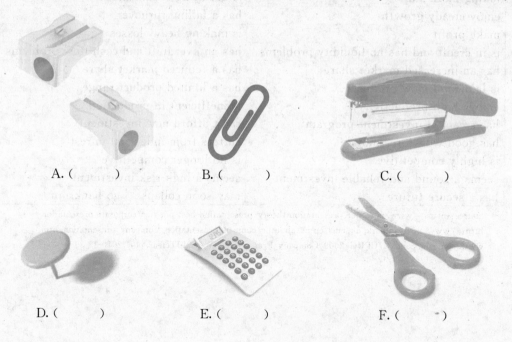

A. (   )   B. (   )   C. (   )

D. (   )   E. (   )   F. (   )

Task 2   Matching.

Match the English words and phrases with their Chinese counterparts.

1. drawing pin/thumb pin   a. 切纸刀
2. pad/post-it   b. 固体胶水
3. book stand   c. 碎纸机
4. photo frame   d. 图钉
5. stapler   e. 便笺本，拍纸簿

6. file holder　　　　　　　　　f. 书立

7. hole punch　　　　　　　　　g. 文件柜

8. binder clip　　　　　　　　　h. 塑封机

9. paper cutter　　　　　　　　i. 相框

10. newspaper rack　　　　　　j. 订书钉

11. marker pen　　　　　　　　k. 文件夹

12. highlighter　　　　　　　　l. 打孔机

13. glue stick　　　　　　　　　m. 长尾夹

14. correction fluid　　　　　　n. 报夹

15. propelling pencil　　　　　　o. 记号笔

16. plastic-envelop machine　　p. 荧光笔

17. document cabinet　　　　　q. 签字笔，中性笔

18. shredder　　　　　　　　　r. 修正液,涂改液

19. gel pen　　　　　　　　　　s. 活页夹

20. binder　　　　　　　　　　t. 自动铅笔

Ⅱ. Introduction to the Topic

Product Presentation

Product presentations are an important part of selling your product to prospective customers. In many cases, this will be the customer's first introduction to your company and potentially your product. First impressions are critical. There are also times when it is important to sell your product to the people inside your company as well as investors. Proper preparation is vital to presenting your product in the best light possible.

The objective of the product presentation is different depending upon the target audience and the presentation should be adjusted accordingly. It is important to know your audience and why they are interested enough to hear your presentation.

Product Presentation Checklist

– Identify Objective

– Identify Target Audience

– Identify the Point of the Presentation

– Include Positioning

– Include Company Overview

– Include Product Description

– Include Benefits

– Include Examples

– Identify and Include Closing Argument

– Can slides be read from across the room?

– Do you need speaker notes?

– Is the presentation proprietary?

– Are there handouts to be included?

Outline of the Product Presentation

The following is a basic outline for a product presentation. You will note that the maximum number of slides is twenty, and fifteen slides is the appropriate number. It is important to keep your presentation precise.

(1) Introduction—Introduce yourself and the points of the product presentation. (1 – 2 slides)

(2) Company Information—This is to make the audience familiar with your company. You can include customer lists, high-profile executives or advisors, information on funding (if a private company), awards and major milestones. Don't spend too much time on this if you don't want your audience to fall asleep. (1 – 5 slides)

(3) Positioning—Successful products have a unique technology or positioning that sets them apart from other products on the market. You should tell how your product is different. This should be done in terms of the problem that they have and that you are solving with your product. This part of your presentation must be very crisp and to the point. (1 – 5 slides)

(4) Product description—Clearly describe your product in terms that your audience will understand. Show how your product fits into their existing environment and interfaces with other products or systems they may be using. (1 – 2 slides)

(5) Clearly state benefits as they relate to your target audience—You can use a features and benefits list. Do not forget the benefits! They may be obvious to you, but your audience will not realize. (1 – 5 slides)

(6) Examples/successes—At this point in the presentation your audience should be familiar with your product and why it is different and better. In order to drive this point home, use examples of how your product is being used and how customers have benefited from the product. (1 – 3 slides)

(7) Closing argument—Summarize your product presentation, reiterate the point of the presentation.

When You are the Presenter

Practice your presentation. No one ever has the time to do it, but even if you are used to winging presentations, the following are the benefits of practice:

(1) Your pitch will be more powerful, polished, and professional.

(2) You are more likely to accomplish your objective.

(3) You look better.

(4) You will get some great suggestions from people who have a slightly different perspective.

Other helpful hints:

– Use gestures to make things visual and clear.

– Use an expressive voice to emphasize points and show your enthusiasm for your product.

– Always stand, even when you are talking to a small audience. Standing projects more energy.

– Use highlights or colors on charts to emphasize an important point. (Though don't over use this, and don't use red unless you want to set off alarms.)

– Use controversy—It is sometimes useful to start your presentation with a controversial statement to grab your audience's attention.

– Use metaphors to help with visualization.

– Make sure you have a smooth verbal transition between slides for a very polished presentation. (This is where the practice really pays off.)

Exercise: True or False

1. _____ Before you present your products, you should introduce you company in details.

2. _____ In your presentation, you should focus on how your products are different from others.

3. _____ In order to make yourself understood, you should not describe your product with too many difficult terms.

4. _____ When presenting, the presenter should stand straight, without using any gestures.

5. _____ The more colors on the chart, the better.

Samples of product presentation[①]

Ladies and Gentlemen,

Good morning. I'm Susan from Deli Group. Today I feel honored to briefly present our company and its products to you.

DELI Group is a professional office supply manufacturer, office supply wholesaler in China. We mainly manufacture office supplies such as file holder, pencil sharpener, paper punch, paper cutter, file box, etc.

More than 20 years experience makes us clearly know how to satisfy customers' requirements of office supplies. In order to ensure the quality of our file holder, pencil sharpener,

---

① http://www.deli-stationery.com/en/index.php,2010-12-30

paper punch, paper cutter, file box, etc. , Deli established its own research and development centers. In addition to advanced production and design technology, Deli also implements a strict quality control system, overseeing each step, from raw material to production lines. Our raw materials adopt imported Korean PP material, German ink and Switzerland nibs, etc. As a result, our office supplies have received ISO 9001—2001 and ISO 14001 certificates. They are commonly used in America, Japan, Germany, and the UK as well as many other parts of the world.

Deli Group is located in Ningbo, a port city of China. This location offers us convenient transportation and also contributes to our low product price. As an office supply manufacturer and wholesaler, Deli promises to provide you high quality and beautifully designed file holder, pencil sharpener and paper punch to customers. If you use Deli office supplies, you will be satisfied with your increased working efficiency.

Now let's have a look at our main products.

Lever Clip File—Office File(File Keeper)

Features of Lever clip file

-Material: Imported environmental protective PP material from Korea.

-These lever arch files have beautiful and bright colors.

-Our file folders have a wide range of styles for your option.

-Customer-oriented design: single fold with several inside pockets.

-The lever clip file is durable and neat.

-The lever clip file has different kinds of clip types for your option.

Applications of Lever clip file

-Lever clip file, a commonly used office supplies, is widely used in offices of enterprises, schools and other organizations.

-A document folder is obviously mainly used to keep files and archives etc.

Arch Binder—Office File(File Keeper)

Features of Arch Binde

-Material: Composite of high quality PVC and imported paper board.

-Good toughness, strong, and neat, durable.

-The design of high-quality metal ring hole facilitates the extraction.

-Colorful labels are available inside the PP ring binder which offers convenient index.

-Beautiful colors and styles.

Applications of Arch Binder

-This kind of office supplies is suitable for keeping and managing different kinds of files in enterprises etc.

-Our arch binders are reliable office supplies. Choose them and you will be convinced by their high quality.

Numbering Machine—Office Stationery(Desk Stationery)

Descriptions of Numbering Machine

-High quality steel is adopted.

-Numbering machines with variety of specifications can be provided: 6 - 15 numbers.

-Simple operation.

-Clear printing.

Applications of Numbering Machine

Numbering machinese are widely used to print date or numbers on files and other objects.

Pencil Sharpener—Office Stationery(Desk Stationery)

Descriptions of Pencil Sharpener

-Material: High quality ABS, so the pencil sharpener has a long service life.

-There are three different types of pencil sharpeners for different groups of people: Q type pencil sharpeners for various kinds of needs; D type pencil is suitable for pencils of different sizes; Business type pencil sharpener for office users.

-Our manual pencil sharpeners can be used for more than 5,000 times.

Whiteboard—Office Appliance(Office products)

Descriptions of White Board

-Whiteboard is a kind of essential supplies.

Deli, as a office supplies manufacturer, can also provide lots of whiteboard accessories: whiteboard frame, whiteboard marker and whiteboard eraser etc.

-Plastic whiteboard frame, MDF whiteboard frame, wodden and aluminum whiteboard frame can all be provided.

Specifications of Whiteboard:

300×450mm to 12,000×18,000mm

Desktop Calculator—Office Appliance

Features of Desktop calculators

-Imported glasses are adopted to make the conductive paper and display device: so the desktop calculator has a clear digital-displaying.

-The keystrokes are made of silica gel, so the keystrokes of our desktop calculators have good resilience and easy to push.

-Double-buttery calculator, durable.

-Convenient to carry for the compact size.

Descriptions of Desktop Calculators:

Deli calculators can be classified into Pocket Calculator, Desktop Calculator and Scientific Calculator etc.

Sealing Tape(PET，BOPP)—Office Appliance(Adhesives)

Descriptions of Sealing Tape

-Material, PET，BOPP.

-High viscosity, good climate adaptive capability.

-Color printing sealing tapes are also available, color printing.

-Sealing tapes can also transmit some information.

Applications of Sealing Tape

Sealing tapes are suitable for sealing various packaging cartons etc. Company's logo or some other information can also be printed on color printing sealing tapes to transmit information.

Thanks very much for your listening. Now is the question time. If you have any questions about our products, please don't hesitate to ask.

Ⅲ. Situational Dialogue

Dialogue 1

At a trade fair，a supermarket buyer from Europe talks to Susan from Deli Group.

Susan: Can I help you, sir?

Buyer: I'd like some information about your pencil sharpener.

Susan: OK. What would you like to know?

Buyer: What's your most popular model?

Susan: Well, our most popular model is A215. Here, this one. As you can see, it looks good, and the price is reasonable.

Buyer: What's the target market?

Susan: It's for white collars, especially business people.

Buyer: I see. How many colors?

Susan: It comes in 3 colors— red, yellow and green. The yellow one is the best seller.

Buyer: Does it have any special features?

Susan: Yes, it's user-friendly design. Try it and you will see it's easy to operate.

Buyer: Hmm, how much is it?

Susan: The trade price is £1.

Buyer: Good. One more question: what about delivery?

Susan: We can deliver within a week.

Buyer: Thanks a lot for your information.

Dialogue 2

A: What's the unit price?

B: It has been selling for a 10% discount since last week. It's only $0.8 now.

A: It's still expensive.

B: Yes, it's not cheap, but I'm sure it's the best sharpener you will ever find.

A: Have you got any desktop calculator?

B: Yes. We have some very stylish desktop calculator.

A: How big are they?

B: They come in different sizes.

A: How much is it?

B: The list price is $10, but you can have it now for $8.5. It's on sale.

A: That's not bad! I'll probably take it.

B: Would you like to place an order now?

A: Oh, no, not yet. I need to look more before I order.

Dialogue 3

A: Is there anything I can do for you?

B: I'm very interested in your whiteboard. How big is it?

A: It's quite big in size, about 50 inches long, 40 inches wide and 60 inches high.

B: Well, that sounds like what I want. Can you give discounts for bulk? I want to buy 2000 of them.

A: In that case, we can cut the price to $5.

B: That's about a 10% discount. Right?

A: Yes.

B: Can the price be lower?

A: Sorry. That's the lowest price we can offer.

B: I have to give it a second thought. Maybe I'll drop in this afternoon. Thank you.

A: My pleasure.

Ⅳ. Practice

Before the class, you should study the products of the relevant companies mentioned below, and jot down all the important information.

In the class, make dialogues according to the following situations, with the information you get beforehand.

Practice 1

Student A: You are Wang Ling, secretary to the Sales manager of Firs Group, a garment manufacturer. You are receiving guests at the trade fair.

Student B: You are a buyer from a European fashion chain store. You are interested in the products of Firs Group. So you stop by its exhibition hall and ask about related questions.

Practice 2

Student A: You are Bill Smith, Purchasing Manager of a supermarket chain. You think the headphones of Edifier Company will sell well, but you want to cut down the price by 2%.

Student B: You are Li Fang, secretary to the Sales Manager of Edifier Company. You are receiving Bill Smith. You agree to give a discount of 2% on the condition that the order must be above 50,000.

Practice 3

Student A: You are David Brown, a buyer of a supermarket chain in Europe. You think the price of staplers from Deli Stationery is quite competitive, but the shapes will not appeal to the European people. So you want to know whether Deli Stationery agrees to produce with customers' samples.

Student B: You are Liu Ying, secretary to the Sales Manager of Deli Stationery. You are receiving David Brown. You agree to process with customers' samples, but the price will go up by 5%.

Ⅴ. Course Project

Paul King, CEO of Officemate Trading Co., Ltd. in Great Britain, is paying a business visit to Great Stationery Co., Ltd.

Mr. Zhang, president of Great Stationery Co., Ltd., asks Rachel to receive Paul King and introduce the products.

Task 1

Rachel is discussing the things to note when presenting the products with Mr. Han Lin, the office dean.

Task 2

Rachel is introducing the products of Great Stationery Co. , Ltd. to Paul King, with the use of PPT.

Task 3

Rachel is comparing the products of Great Stationery Co. , Ltd. and those of their rival company Roy Maximum.

Project 16
Business Dinners

Task 1 Picture recognition.

Can you name the following table wares?

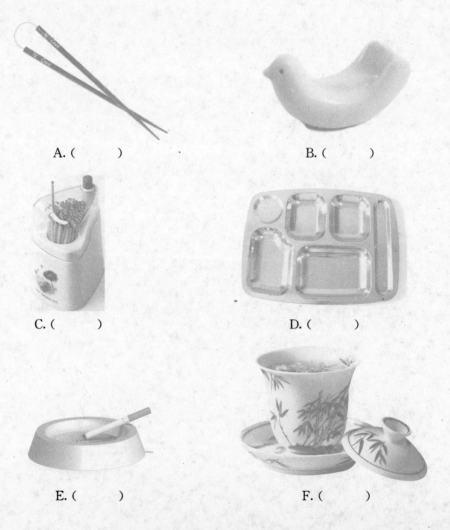

A. (   )

B. (   )

C. (   )

D. (   )

E. (   )

F. (   )

Task 2   Matching.

Match the English words and phrases with their Chinese counterparts.

1. finger bowl	a. 餐桌用具
2. hand towel	b. 桌布
3. serving tray	c. 吸管
4. vinegar bottle	d. 小碟子
5. coffee pot	e. 餐巾
6. straw	f. 纸巾
7. table ware	g. 小毛巾
8. serving-cart/serving trolley	h. 咖啡壶
9. paper napkin/tissues	i. 洗手盅
10. saucer	j. 银筷子
11. champagne cooler	k. 烟灰缸
12. napkin	l. 托盘
13. ice tong	m. 烛架
14. salt shaker	n. 胡椒粉罐
15. sliver chopsticks	o. 盐瓶
16. ashtray	p. 醋瓶
17. table cloth	q. 服务餐车
18. pepper pot	r. 面包篮
19. candle stick	s. 香槟桶
20. bread basket	t. 小冰块夹

Ⅱ. Introduction to the Topic

Business Dining Etiquette

Dining Etiquette has always played an important part in making a favorable impression. Our actions at the table and while eating therefore, can be essential to how others perceive us and can even affect our professional success in the business world.

Pre-Dinner Etiquette

When making the initial invitation, make sure each guest is aware of the purpose of the gathering. Let people know what to expect.

Arrive early! As the host, you should be the first person present. Arriving early can also give you time to check the table and the menu before greeting any guests. Be sure there is adequate seating and introduce yourself to the waiter who will be serving you. If you are hosting business clients, you will pay for the meal. This can be established before any guests arrive so the wait staff can avoid potentially embarrassing questions later.

Wait by the door so you are able to greet guests as they arrive and escort them to the table, or have the waiter or waitress show your guests to the table where you will be waiting for them. It is best not to order anything to eat or drink while you are waiting to greet all your guests.

Sitting Down
When guests arrive, introduce them to one another and show them where you would like them to sit.

As a guest, you should not sit in your seat until your host or hostess has done so. If there is no host, then you should wait for the senior or oldest person at the table to sit first before you sit in your seat.

Do not place any bags, purses, sunglasses, cell phones, or briefcases on the table.

When you are all seated, gently unfold your napkin and place it on your lap, folded in half with the fold towards your waist.

Keep utensils in the same order they appear on the table.

Wait for all parties to arrive before beginning any part of the meal.

Place Setting
Solids on your left:
-Forks
-Butter plate
-Napkin (may also be on your plate)
Liquids on your right:
-Glasses/Cups
-Knives
-Spoons
● Whether basic or formal place setting, use your utensils from the outside in.
● Dessert utensils may be above the place setting or served with dessert.

Eating Styles
Continental or *European* style: cutting the food with the right hand and using the left hand to hold the food while cutting and when eating.
American style: cutting the food with the right hand and holding the food with the left, then switching hands to eat with the right hand.

Starting the Meal
When all the guests are present, it is the duty of the host to "call the meal to order". This can simply be a statement indicating that everyone is present and it is time to begin the meal and get down to business.

The host sets the tone for the meal. If the host orders alcohol, other guests will feel free to

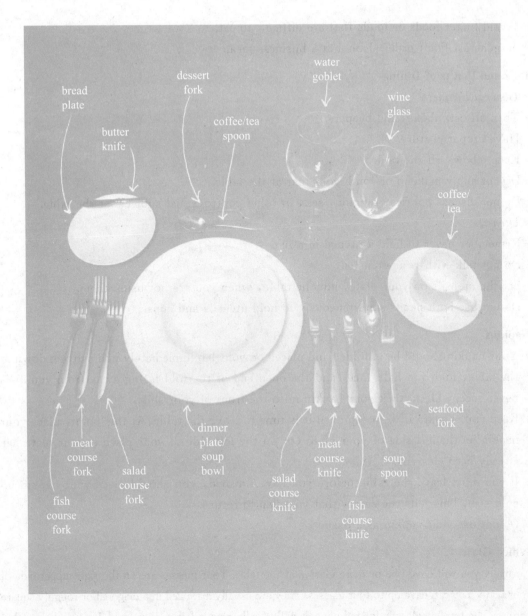

do so as well. If you intend for guests to order appetizers, you must begin by ordering one yourself. The same is true for dessert.

All good guests will wait for the host to begin. Don't keep them waiting. If it is a small gathering, wait until everyone has been served. If you are hosting a larger gathering, it is only necessary to wait until several people have been served their food. If you are not served near the beginning, you may tell your guests to go ahead while their food is still hot.

Ordering
- When in doubt, follow the lead of the host.
- Don't order the most expensive item.
- Order simply.

- Avoid finger foods or foods that are difficult to eat.
- In general, don't order alcohol at a business meal.

Do's and Don'ts of Dining

- *General Etiquette*
- Turn off cell phones and beepers.
- Have proper posture.
- Keep elbows off the table.
- Do not apply makeup or comb your hair at the table.
- Do not discuss politics, religion, sex, or other controversial subjects at the table.
- *Utensils*
- Remember never to hold a utensil in a fist.
- Do not talk with your utensils.
- Set the utensils on your plate, not the table, when you are not using them.
- Do not use both hands simultaneously to hold utensils and cups.

Napkins

- Your napkin should be unfolded and placed on your lap immediately upon sitting down at the table, folded in half once, and the open end of the fold facing away from you. It is never acceptable to tuck your napkin in to the front of your shirt.
- Keep your napkin in your lap until it is time to leave the table. At this point, place your napkin on the left side of your plate (or on the left side of your place if your plate has already been cleared).
- If you must leave the table before you have finished, you should place your napkin on your seat. This tells the server that you plan to return.
- Do not use your napkin as a tissue

Which Glass

Normally you will have two or more glasses at the table. Your glasses are on the right upper side of your plate. You can have up to four glasses. They are usually arranged in a diagonal or roughly square pattern. The top left glass is for red wine. It will usually have a fairly large bowl. Directly below that you will find the white wine glass, which will be smaller. At the top right, you will find a champagne glass. Your water glass is on the bottom right.

While Eating
- Don't talk with your mouth full.
- If you have to sneeze, turn your head away from the table.
- Take small bites.
- Cut your salad into bite size pieces if necessary.
- When eating soup, don't put the whole spoon in to your mouth. Bring the spoon to your mouth and drink the soup from the edge of the spoon. If the soup is hot, gently stir your soup to cool it instead of blowing on it. And, of course, do not slurp.

–You should always use both your knife and fork together. You should not cut your food up at the start and then use your fork only. You should only cut one edible piece of meat at a time.

– Try to pace yourself to finish at the same time as everyone else.

– If you leave the table, excuse yourself and place your napkin on your seat.

– When you have finished eating, place your napkin neatly to the left of your plate, but do not push your place setting away from you.

After Dinner

● Thank each guest for attending and acknowledge each one individually as he or she departs with a handshake or a remark.

● Once all of the guests have left, thank the wait staff that assisted you.

● After all of your guests have left and the bill has been settled, you can leave content knowing you were a gracious host. Cheers!

Exercise: True or False

1. _____ You don't have to wait by the door for guests to arrive.

2. _____ When you sit down, you can put your mobile phone on the table.

3. _____ Politics is not a good topic for conversation during the meal.

4. _____ If you place your napkin on your seat, it means you haven't finished your meal.

5. _____ If you want to leave the table, you should do it quietly, without telling anyone.

Ⅲ. Situational Dialogue

Dialogue 1

Susan comes to the hotel to invite Paul to a dinner party.

Susan: Good morning, Paul. How is your room?

Paul: Very comfortable and quiet. I just feel at home.

Susan: I'm glad to hear that. Now, I'm coming to tell you that we'll be having a dinner party tomorrow evening. We'd like to invite you to come.

Paul: Oh, how nice of you! I would be delighted to come. By the way, what time is the dinner?

Susan: 6 o'clock.

Paul: And the place?

Susan: Shipu Restaurant.

Paul: But where is Shipu Restaurant?

Susan: Don't worry. I'll send somebody to pick you up from the hotel at 5:30 tomorrow evening. Will that be convenient for you?

Paul: Yes. That's fine. Thank you.

Susan: See you then.

Paul: See you.

Dialogue 2

Paul enters the restaurant. Susan's boss, Mr. Ding, General Manager of Snow-white Stationery, sees him and greets him.

Ding: Welcome. I'm glad you've come.

Paul: It's very kind of you to have invited me.

Ding: Sit down, please. I hope the food I've ordered will be to your liking.

Paul: Of course I will like it.

(*They sit down and begin to have dinner.*)

Ding: Please help yourself.

Paul: Thank you. I certainly will. All the dishes look splendid.

Ding: You're leaving soon. Has your trip to this fair been fruitful?

Paul: Yes, there's a really wide range of goods on display and most prices are acceptable.

Ding: Have you found anything that particularly interests you?

Paul: Yes. We're interested in your … The designs are original. I'm sure they will be quite popular with your customers in Europe.

Ding: Yes, you are right. They are our latest designs, very popular with students here. I'm sure they will sell well in Europe.

Paul: We hope so.

Ding: All right. May I propose a toast to our continued friendship and cooperation?

Paul: I couldn't agree more. Cheers!

(*They're raising glasses.*)

Dialogue 3　Zhejiang cuisine

Ding: Just as the old saying goes "when in Rome, do as the Romans do". Now, I should say "when in Zhejiang, eat as Zhejiang people eat".

Paul: I'm always interested in tasting local food.

Ding: Do you have any ideas of Zhejiang Cuisine?

Paul: I know nothing about it. Will you be so kind as to introduce it?

Ding: I'm glad to. You know, Zhejiang is regarded as "the land of fish and rice", so Zhejiang Cuisine occupies an important position in Chinese food. It mainly consists of four local styles, Hangzhou, Ningbo, Shaoxing and Wenzhou, each having its own local characteristics.

Paul: Really? What are their respective features?

Ding: Hangzhou Cuisine, the representative of Zhejiang Cuisine, is characterized by its elaborate preparation and varying techniques of cooking, such as sautéing, stewing, and stir- and deep-frying. Hangzhou food tastes fresh and crisp, varying with the change of season. Ningbo food is a bit salty but delicious. Specializing in steamed, roasted and braised seafood, Ningbo cuisine is particular in retaining the original freshness, tenderness and softness. Shaoxing cuisine offers fresh aquatic food and poultry that has a special rural flavor, sweet in smell, soft and glutinous in taste, thick in gravy and strong in season. Wenzhou Cuisine is light on the use of oil, and often uses yellow croaker fish, crab and squid as ingredients.

Paul: Do they have anything in common?

Ding: Yes, of course. They are all characterized by the careful selection of ingredients, emphasizing minute preparation, and unique, fresh and tender tastes.

Paul: Do we try all of them today?

Ding: No. We'll try Hangzhou Cuisine this evening.

Paul: Any famous dishes to recommend?

Ding: Typical of Hangzhou cuisine, such as Hangzhou roast chicken (commonly known as Beggar's chicken), Dongpo pork, West Lake Fish in Vinegar Sauce, Songsao (means "Sister-in-law Song") Shredded Fish Soup.

Paul: I can't wait to eat.

Ⅳ. Practice

Make dialogues according to the following situations.

Practice 1

Student A: Your boss wants to have a welcome dinner with a newly-arrived client and asks you to invite him.

Your boss' name (open)

The client's name (open)

Time (open)

Restaurant (open)

Student B: You are the client. And you accept the invitation pleasantly.

Practice 2

Student A: You are Mr. Li Gang, President of Fox Group. You're having a business dinner with David Brown, Purchasing Manager of a client company.

Student B： You are David Brown. Discuss the cooperation in the near future during the dinner.

Practice 3

Student A： You are the boss of a trade company. Now you are having dinner with a foreigner，one of your clients. Introduce one of the Eight Cuisine in China to him.

Student B： You are the foreigner. You are keen on Chinese food. And you are eager to gain the knowledge of Chinese food.

Ⅴ. Course Project

Paul King，CEO of Officemate Trading Co.，Ltd. in Great Britain，is paying a business visit to Great Stationery Co.，Ltd. Mr. Zhang，president of Great Stationery Co.，Ltd.，wants to hold a business dinner for Mr. Paul King.

Rachel，secretary of Mr. Zhang，who has gone through the new employee training and been familiar with their office environment，is ready to start to work independently.

Task 1

Mr. Zhang asks Rachel to write an invitation card or letter in English with the information given below.

> 日期：2010 年 4 月 15 日（星期四）
> 时间：下午 6 点半
> 地点：宁波市解放南路 188 号，新园宾馆

Sample of invitation card

> Mr. David White
>
> requests the pleasure of the company of
>
> **Mr. & Mrs. Anderson**
>
> at dinner
>
> at 6:00 pm, on Monday，12 May
>
> at Garden Hotel
>
> Tel：77854296
> R. S. V. P. ①
>
> Dress：formal

---

① R. S. V. P.，敬请回复。

Sample of invitation letter

> March 10, 2010
> Dear Mr. David Brown,
> We would like to invite you to a dinner party on Sunday Feb. 11 2007, to be held in the Dainty Restaurant at the Marriott Hotel. This is to welcome Dr Susan.
> Please let us know as soon as possible if you are able to attend this dinner.
>
> Yours sincerely,

Task 2

Mr. Zhang asks Rachel to write a welcome speech for him.

Sample of welcome speech

> Ladies and Gentlemen,
> Today we feel honored to hold a welcome dinner for Mr. Paul King, the CEO of Officemate Trading Co., Ltd. First of all, allow me, on behalf of the company, to extend a warm welcome to our distinguished guest.
>
> You know, Officemate Trading Co., Ltd. has been in business relationship with our company for more than ten years. And we benefit a lot from the cooperation. We believe Mr. Paul King's visit will improve the understanding of each other and strengthen the cooperation, thus lead to an even brighter future to both companies.
>
> Mr. Paul King will stay in Ningbo for one week. He will visit our factories, discuss the details of deeper cooperation, especially broadening the market in Europe in the near future.
>
> Finally, I'd like to express our sincere welcome again and hope that Mr. Paul King will have a wonderful time in Ningbo.

Task 3

During the farewell dinner, Paul King gives a farewell speech. Mr. Zhang asks Rachel to interpret the farewell speech.

The following is the farewell speech

> Ladies and Gentlemen,
> My visit to Ningbo is drawing to a close and I'll leave for Britain tomorrow.
>
> On the eve of my departure, it is a great honor for me to say a few words here to express my appreciation for the hospitality you showed me during my stay in Ningbo. People in your company are hard-working and prudent, which gave me very deep impression. I should say that this visit is quite fruitful and I'm confident that it will be helpful to the further strengthening of our cooperation.
>
> I'm looking for the pleasure of greeting you in Britain in the near future, so that we can push the relationship between us a step forward.
>
> Thank you again. Wish you good health and success!

Project 17

Booking a Hotel Room

Ⅰ. Warming-Up

Task 1   Picture recognition.

Look at the following six pictures and discuss with your partners. Talk about different hotels.

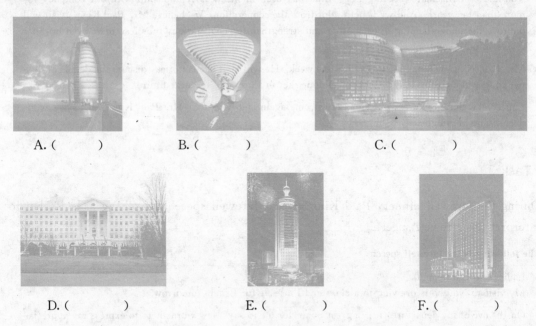

A. (   )   B. (   )   C. (   )

D. (   )   E. (   )   F. (   )

Task 2   Matching.

Match the English words and phrases with their Chinese counterparts.

1. receipt		a. 门厅
2. ashtray		b. 过道
3. bathrobe		c. 走廊
4. dressing table		d. 电梯

5. twin beds　　　　　　　　e. 问询处

6. double bed　　　　　　　　f. 接待室

7. single bed　　　　　　　　g. 登记表

8. built-in wardrobe, closet　h. 休息厅

9. double room　　　　　　　i. 房间号码

10. single room　　　　　　　j. 一套房间

11. suite　　　　　　　　　　k. 单人房间

12. room number　　　　　　　l. 双人房间

13. lounge　　　　　　　　　　m. 壁橱

14. registration form　　　　n. 单人床

15. reception office　　　　　o. 双人床

16. information desk　　　　　p. 成对床

17. lift, elevator　　　　　　q. 浴衣

18. lobby　　　　　　　　　　r. 烟灰缸

19. corridor　　　　　　　　　s. 梳妆台

20. entrance hall　　　　　　t. 收据

Ⅱ. Introduction to the Topic

How to Book a Hotel Room

Introduction

Depending on how you find it, the rate for a single hotel room can vary much. Your job, as a savvy secretary, is to find the best room at the cheapest price for your company. If you go into this process blind, then you are almost always going to pay more. Here are some suggestions on how you can use the powerful Internet—to find the room of and for your dreams.

Step 1—Check price comparison sites

Price comparison websites such as **Google, Yahoo and Baidu** will check multiple websites, including hotel consolidator and booking services, for hotel room prices. They will then tell you the lowest price found.

(1) Go to the websites **Google, Yahoo and Baidu**.

(2) Input the name of the city and your dates of travel into the appropriate fields.

(3) Click on "Search".

(4) Note the lowest price you have found for the hotel(s) you are interested in, as well as the name of the website offering that price.

Step 2—Call the hotel

By calling the hotel directly, you can usually get a lower rate than the one advertised on the web. However, you must call the hotel itself, not the national 800 number, to get these rates.

To look up the phone number of the specific hotels you've noted in Steps 1 and 2, go to **Google Maps** and click on "Find Businesses".

Eg. 1: *Google Maps main page*

(1) Type the name of the hotel into the "What" box.

(2) Type the city the hotel is located in into the "Where" box.

Eg. 2: *Google Maps Find Businesses page*

(1) Click "Search Businesses".

(2) Check to make sure it is the same hotel you found in Steps 1 and 2: some chains have multiple hotels with similar names in the same city.

(3) Call the local number of the hotel. It will be the number that does not have the "800" area code. You will get a better rate by speaking to the hotel directly than by calling their national 800 number.

(4) Ask what their rate is for the dates you wish to stay there.

(5) If you are a frequent guest of a specific hotel chain, booking through the hotel chain will garner points and amenities that booking through a third-party web service will not.

Step 3—Ask for a discount

(1) Always ask for a discount when you speak to the hotel. If they don't offer you a discount, ask them if they will upgrade you to a better class of room at that rate.

(2) While speaking to the hotel, ask, "Is it possible for me to get a discount?" or "I was hoping to pay a little less." Don't say, "I found a better rate on the Web"; they'll just tell you to book it on the Web.

(3) Be nice. The nicer you are, the more likely you are to get a better rate or an upgrade.

(4) Call after the reservation office has closed for the evening; the front desk clerk, if he or she is not busy, is more likely to give you a lower rate than the reservation office or the hotel manager is.

(5) If the clerk is busy, offer to call back; being considerate of the clerk's situation may also help you get a discount.

Step 4—Ask if they will match the lowest rate

(1) Most hotels will match the lowest rate you've found online. Additionally, many chains have programs in which they offer big discounts if you find a rate lower than their lowest rate.

(2) If their lowest rates aren't as low as the one you found online, ask if they will match

the rate you found.

(3) Many chains have a Lowest Rate Guarantee program. If you find a rate lower than the lowest one they offer on their website, they will give you an even more deeply discounted rate.

Some Lowest Rate Guarantees in the USA

Intercontinental Hotels: Lowest Internet Rate Guarantee 10% off any rate lower than their lowest rate.

Best Western: Low Rate, GUARANTEED! Find a lower rate, get an additional 10% discount.

Harrah's Entertainment, Inc. : Harrah's Best Rate Guarantee find a lower rate, get additional 25% off (includes Caesars).

Radisson Hotels & Resorts: Best Online Rate Find lower rate, get additional 25% off.

Days Inn: Get the guaranteed best hotel rate or your first night is free.

Ramada: Get the guaranteed best hotel rate or your first night is free.

Travelodge: Get the guaranteed best hotel rate or your first night is free.

Choice Hotels: Best Internet Rates Guarantee Find a better rate, get 10% off.

Hyatt: Best Rate Guarantee find a lower rate and Hyatt will beat it by 20%.

Starwood Hotels & Resorts: The Best Rates. Guaranteed. 10% off a better rate or 2,000 Starpoints—includes Westin, Sheraton, Le Meridien, W, St. Regis.

Wyndham Hotels & Resorts: Webmatch Match best rate, plus first night free.

Orbitz: Low Price Guarantee Will refund the difference between their rate and the lowest rate.

Expedia: The Expedia Best Price Guarantee Will refund the difference and give you a $50 travel coupon.

Hilton Hotels: Our Best Rates. Guaranteed. Find a lower rate, get a $50 American Express Gift Check.

Conclusion

While there are many sites on the Internet that will tell you that you can get the best rate through them, in the end, the best way to get a hotel room cheap is to do some searching on your own. Nothing beats the persuasive power of a phone call to the hotel itself. Remember: it never hurts to ask. Of course, you can also make out like a bandit by bidding on the room you want. No hotel wants their beds empty.

Exercise: True or False

1. _____ If you want to book a hotel room, just call the manager of the hotel.

2. _____ When you book a hotel room, always tell the clerk that you are a frequent guest.

3. _____ Searching on the internet, you can always get a best rate of the hotel room.

4. _____ The hotel advertisement always tell the true price.

5. _____ The front desk clerks in a hotel are always helpful.

Ⅲ. Situational Dialogue

Dialogue 1   Reserve a hotel room

Mr. Green is phoning Hotel clerk to book a hotel room. The following dialogue is between Mr. Green and Hotel clerk.

Clerk：Hello. Holiday Inn. May I help you?

Green：Yes, I'd like to reserve a room for two on the 21st of March.

Clerk：OK. Let me check our books here for a moment. The 21st of May, right?

Green：No. March, not May.

Clerk：Oh, sorry. Let me see here. Hmmm.

Green：Are you all booked that night?

Clerk：Well, we do have one suite available, with a sauna bath. And the view of the sea is great, too.

Green：How much is that?

Clerk：It's only $200 dollars.

Green：Oh, that's a little too expensive for me. Do you have a cheaper room available either on the 20th or the 22nd?

Clerk：Well, would you like a smoking or a non-smoking room?

Green：Non-smoking, please.

Clerk：OK, we do have a few rooms available on the 20th; we're full on the 22nd, unless you want a smoking room.

Green：Well, how much is the non-smoking room on the 20th?

Clerk：$80 dollars.

Green：OK, that'll be fine.

Clerk：All right. Could I have your name, please?

Green：Yes. Jim Green.

Clerk：How do you spell your last name, Mr. Green?

Green：G-R-E-E-N.

Clerk：OK, Mr. Green, we look forward to seeing you on March 20th.

Green：OK. Goodbye.

Dialogue 2   Arriving a hotel

Mr. Green arrived at the hotel.

Clerk： Good morning, Sir.

Green： Good morning, my name is Green. I called you a couple of days ago to make a reservation.

Clerk： Oh, yes, Mr. Green, a double room with sauna bath.

Green： That's me.

Clerk： And you have booked two nights.

Green： That's right.

Clerk： Here's your key, Mr. Green. Room 504. It's on the fifth floor. There's a lift on your right. Have a nice evening.

Green： Thank you.

Dialogue 3   Checking out of a hotel

Clerk： Good morning. May I help you?

Green： ·Yes, I'd like to check out now. My name is Green, room 504. Here is the key.

Clerk： One moment, please, sir. Here's your bill. Would you like to check and see if the amount is correct?

Green： What's the 17 dollars for?

Clerk： That's for the phone calls you made from your room.

Green： Can I pay with ID card?

Clerk： Certainly. May I have your passport, please?

Green： Here you are.

Clerk： Could you sign your name here for me?

Green： Sure.

Clerk： Here is your receipt, Sir. Thank you.

Green： Thank you. Goodbye.

Ⅳ. Practice

Practice 1   Booking a hotel room

Make a dialogue according to the following information.

Student A： Your boss wants to meet a client in Shenzhen and asks you to book a hotel room for both; him and the client. They will stay in Shenzhen for three days. Your boss is a non-smoker. Book a hotel room according to the following information.

Your boss' name (open)

The client's name (open)

The hotel telephone number

The date of the meeting (open)

Student B: You are the Clerk of Shinning Pearl Hotel. Student A would like to book a hotel room for two persons, but one is a smoker, another is a non-smoker. Make sure you get the following information:

– Name and telephone number of the two guests.

– The days that they will stay.

– The special requests your guests asked.

Practice 2　Check in the hotel

Student A: You are the boss from Good Luck Trade Company. Your secretary has booked the hotel room for you. Now check in the hotel.

Student B: You are a Hotel clerk in Shenzhen Shinning Pearl Hotel. Receive the guests who had made a reservation in your hotel.

Practice 3　Checking out a hotel

Student A: You had finished your business stay in the hotel, now check out of the hotel, but there is some extra expense (78 $) that you don't know. Ask the hotel clerk for explanation.

Student B: You are the hotel clerk. The guests are leaving the hotel, but they have something puzzling. Please give them a reasonable explanation.

Ⅴ. Course Project

You are on business with your boss to take part in the 100th Chinese Export Commodities Fair in Guangzhou. You have made a reservation with the White Swan Hotel.

Task 1

On the way from the airport to the hotel, your boss is asking something about the hotel and the arrangement you have made. Now give a full description of the White Swan Hotel and the arrangement you have made.

Task 2

After checking in the hotel, your boss wants to meet an important client from the Middle East discussing the cooperation. Please contact the Front Desk and arrange a meeting room for your boss.

Booking Tickets

Task 1　Picture recognition.

Look at the following 6 pictures which are the top airlines in the world, then work in pairs to talk about the airlines you like. You can refer to the information given below.

A.

Singapore Airlines may be based in a small country, but it covers a lot of international destinations and flies more passengers every year than the entire population of Singapore.

B.

Cathay Pacific is also a member of the One World Alliance and is the top ranked Asian-based airline by Skytrax.

C.

Qantas is a member of Oneworld, alongside British Airways, and repeatedly scores well with passengers around the world for its service.

D.

Thai Airways is the top ranked airline affiliated with Star Alliance. Thai is known for its inflight service, and its flight attendants wear traditional Thai clothing during their flights.

E.

Asiana Airlines is part of Star Alliance, and flies to over 50 cities in 17 countries.

F.

The red and blue in the logo of Malaysia Airlines is said to represent equilibrium.

Task 2　Matching.

Match the English words and phrases with their Chinese counterparts.

1. aircraft crew, air crew	a. 连续飞行
2. pilot	b. 航线
3. steward	c. 客机
4. stewardess, hostess	d. 机场主楼
5. passenger plane	e. 男服务员
6. Airbus	f. 舱口
7. hatch	g. 空中客车
8. main airport building, terminal building	h. 空中小姐
9. air route, air line	i. 驾驶员，机长
10. non-stop flight	j. 着陆
11. airsick	k. 起飞
12. direct flight, straight flight	l. 颠簸
13. landing	m. 机组，机务人员
14. to rock, to toss, to bump	n. 直飞
15. to take off, take-off	o. 晕机

Ⅱ. Introduction to the Topic

How to Book Airline Tickets

Instructions

Step 1: Start your search on the internet at least 21 days ahead of time. Arrange your travel midweek and stay over a Saturday night whenever possible. It would be much cheaper. The cheap seats always sell out first.

Step 2: Look for flights on your frequent-flier carrier first and compare its cheapest rate to those on sites. Also check out consolidators and auction sites. Many airline Web sites offer lower Internet-only fares.

Step 3: Consider flying through a big city airport. Because there many more flights than the small city.

Step 4: Request your seat preference (aisle or window) when buying your ticket. You could find yourself with a middle seat if you wait until check-in.

Step 5: Request any special assistance or equipment (such as a wheelchair) for disabled travelers prior to arriving at the airport.

Step 6: Keep the length of the flight, the layovers, the amount of gear you're carrying and the time of day in mind when deciding whether to buy a seat (often discounted) for an infant. Domestic carriers permit you to hold children under 2 years of age on your lap, while international flights require a ticket and a seat for every passenger.

Step 7: Find out whether tickets are refundable, transferable or changeable (and at what cost) before you buy. Get e-tickets when possible. Having paper tickets mailed usually involves an extra fee.

Tips & Warnings

−Join a frequent-flier program if you haven't yet. Even if you fly on a bunch of different airlines, the miles will eventually add up.

−If your favorite airline doesn't go to your destination, ask if it has reciprocity with another airline.

Exercise: True or False

1. _____It is the best way to book the cheapest ticket on the internet.
2. _____ If you can't find the cheap ticket, just go to the airport to buy the ticket.
3. _____ The earlier you book the ticket ahead of your travel time, the cheaper tickets you can get.
4. _____ You can always book the cheaper tickets on the internet.
5. _____ It is cheaper to book a seat in the front of the passenger cabin.

III. Situational Dialogue

Dialogue 1 Booking a ticket

Mr. Green is phoning Reservations clerk to book a plane ticket. The following dialogue is between Mr. Green and Reservation clerk.

Clerk: Southeast Airways, good morning. May I help you?

Green: Yes, do you have any flights to Shenzhen next Wednesday afternoon?

Clerk: One moment, please...Yes. There's a flight at 16:45 and one at 18:00.

Green: That's fine. Could you tell me how much a return flight costs? I'll be staying three weeks.

Clerk: Economy, business class or first class ticket?

Green: Economy, please.

Clerk: That would be 780RMB.

Green: OK. Could I make a reservation?

Clerk: Certainly. Which flight would you like?

Green: The 16:45, please.

Clerk: Could I have your name, please?

Green: My name is Jim Green, that's J-I-M, G-R-E-E-N.

Clerk: How would you like to pay, Mr. Green?

Green: Can I pay at the check-in desk when I pick up my ticket?

Clerk: Yes, but you will have to confirm this reservation at least two hours before departure time.

Green: I see.

Clerk: Now you have been booked, Mr. Green. The flight leaves at 16:45, and your arrival in Shenzhen will be at 18:45 p. m. The flight number is MU5812.

Green: Thank you.

Dialogue 2 Confirmation of flight reservation

Before the arrival at the airport.

Clerk: Southeast Airlines. Can I help you?

Green: Hello. I'd like to reconfirm my flight, please.

Clerk: May I have your name and flight number, please?

Green: My name is Green, Jim Green, and my flight number is MU5812.

Clerk: When are you leaving?

Green: 16:45, On June 12th.

Clerk: And your destination?

Green：Shenzhen.

Clerk：Hold the line, please. (...) All right. Your seat is confirmed, Mr. Green. You'll be arriving in Shenzhen at 18：45 o'clock p. m. local time.

Green：Thank you. Can I pick up my ticket when I check in?

Clerk：Yes, but please check in at least two hours before departure time.

Dialogue 3　At passport control

Immigration Officer：Good evening. Where have you come from?

Zhang：　　　　　　　　Hangzhou, China.

Immigration Officer：May I have your passport, please?

Zhang：　　　　　　　　Here you are.

Immigration Officer：What's the nature of your visit? Business or pleasure?

Zhang：　　　　　　　　Pleasure. I'm visiting my relatives.

Immigration Officer：How long are you going to stay in Canada?

Zhang：　　　　　　　　Three weeks.

Immigration Officer：What is your occupation?

Zhang：　　　　　　　　I work as a technician for a China telecommunications company.

Immigration Officer：Do you have a return ticket?

Zhang：　　　　　　　　Yes, here it is.

Immigration Officer：That's fine. Thanks. Enjoy your trip.

Zhang：　　　　　　　　Thank you.

Ⅳ. Practice

Practice 1　Booking a plane ticket

Make a dialogue according to the following information.

Student A：Your boss and the other workmates want to fly to New York in a month to visit an international stationary fair and ask you to book the tickets for them. They will stay in New York for seven days. Now, book three return tickets according to the following information.

Your boss' name (open)

Your workmates' name (open)

Destination：New York

The date of departure：May 15

Student B：You are the Clerk of Southeast Airlines. Student A would like to book tickets for three person to New York. Make sure you get the following information：

- Name and telephone number of the three guests.

- The date of their departure.

– The special requests your guests asked.

Practice 2   Conforming the flight ticket

Student A: Your boss and your workmates will leave for New York the next day. Before leaving, you are making a confirmation of flight reservation.

Student B: You are a reservations clerk of Southeast Airlines. Receive the guests who had made a reservation in your Airlines.

Practice 3   At passport control

Student A: You are the immigration officer in the United States and you are checking the person who is visiting the relatives in United States. You should get the following information.

The purpose of visiting United States

The time stayed in United states

The nationality, the name and the occupation of the visitor

Student B: You are the visitor who is visiting the United States. Your English is not very well, and your English puzzled the immigration officer. Furthermore, you cannot find the return ticket. Please give him a reasonable explanation.

V. Course Project

You are going to Hamburg to attend a stationary exhibition with your boss. You have taken large luggage with you, including computers, catalogues, clothes, foods and so on.

Task 1

When you arrived at the Customs and claimed your luggage, some problems appeared. The Customs Officer had found some powder and liquids in your luggage. Now, give an explanation to the Customs Officer.

Task 2

Now you have arrived Hamburg Airport, you found that nobody had come to meet you as expected. What will you do in this strange world.

Task 3

After the Exhibition, your boss wants to visit some of the interest places in Germany. You have three days stay there. Now make a plan for your boss, including places you will visit and the recreations your boss wants to enjoy.